T0375479

True Success

A Novel

Dale E. Best

WESTBOW
PRESS®
A DIVISION OF THOMAS NELSON
& ZONDERVAN

WestBow Press books may be ordered through booksellers or by contacting:

WestBow Press
A Division of Thomas Nelson & Zondervan
1663 Liberty Drive
Bloomington, IN 47403
www.westbowpress.com
844-714-3454

ISBN: 979-8-3850-1851-2 (sc)
ISBN: 979-8-3850-1852-9 (hc)
ISBN: 979-8-3850-1853-6 (e)

Library of Congress Control Number: 2024902506

Print information available on the last page.

WestBow Press rev. date: 03/12/2024

Contents

Prologue

"A successful life is a life of action not inaction."
The Power of Being Different

~ **By John Paul Carcinci**

Harry McKenzie was raised with his two brothers in the bustling town of Evansville in the southwest corner of Indiana. Of the three boys he was the most athletic and learned early about being a team player and excelled in baseball as the pitcher on his Mater Dei High School team. With scholarships and part-time jobs he was able to continue his education, pass the bar exam and become a respected lawyer in his hometown.

During his junior year in college he married his longtime sweetheart, Gemme, and they became a dynamic couple capable of sharing their lives with many people in many different ways.

Gemme was raised as an only child with a strong talent for helping others from the time she was a young girl, regardless of their station in life. She and Harry found themselves well matched in this regard in their life together.

Harry's desire to help others guided his legal work when he joined the Law Office of Fleming & Johnson after college as a senior clerk with the goal of making full partner. Little did he and Gemme realize the toll this goal would take and the turns their lives would make as they faced the diverse demands they were presented.

Caring for others, though often painful and expensive, became their mission when their lives were forcibly altered from their original path.

Author's Note

PURE SUCCESS is a work of fiction. The characters are imaginary. Some of the events in the story take place in real towns and cities that have been selected to fictitiously enhance the story. Any similarity to actual persons, living or dead, is purely coincidental and not the intent of the author.

1

Fleming & Johnson Law Firm

> "Ideas don't come out fully formed. They only become clear as you work on them. You just have to get started."
>
> ~ **Mark Zuckerberg**

It's a beautiful spring day as Harry stepped out of the apartment in Evansville, Indiana. Harry was whistling as he walked from the edge of the parking lot to his first day of work at the Fleming & Johnson Law office on Green River Road.

Harry was proud to begin his job as an attorney. His mom's brother, Uncle Tom had some pull and got him the job. Harry was looking dapper with his suit, white shirt, and bold red and blue striped tie. He was recalling what his mom drilled into him in high school. Dress like the person in the position you want to be. Mr. Fleming's job was his goal for now. Harry's shoulders were square, and waist was narrow. By his build, one could tell he had been a member of his Mater Dei High School state champion baseball team.

He continued whistling as he rounded the corner of the office at his new job. He pulled firmly on the large glass door and confidently strolled in remembering politeness wins friends.

Earlier, Harry had been introduced to the secretary, Gladys. "Good morning, Gladys." In college, he had formed the habit of speaking first and presenting a cordial attitude.

She replied, "Harry, good morning. It is nice to have you on our team." As Harry walked on, she trailed off with, "Have a good day."

Harry kept a fairly even stride as he walked toward Mr. Fleming's desk. As he approached, Mr. Fleming arose, so Harry reached out his hand and offered to shake his boss' hand. Mr. Fleming met his hand and gave a firm handshake. After this quick greeting, Mr. Fleming got down to business.

"Harry, I'm working on a case and I really need a precedent to present to the jury and the presiding judge. Would you go in the research room and do that for me?"

"Yes, sir," Harry affirmed. He ambled off with the synopsis of the case in his hand. Hopefully, this wouldn't be too hard since he had to do some of this in law school. He checked the indices in two different sets of law books to find a suitable one. Before he realized it, Gladys poked her head in and asked, "Harry, do you want to take a coffee break with us?"

"Yes, Ma'am," he answered as he placed a slip of paper in the law book to hold his place.

Gladys introduced him to all the personnel in the office with varying degrees of responsibility to the law firm. The first day was going great.

Before the day was over, he did find two precedents. One fit perfectly and one would need an explanation to the jury to fit the case.

Harry felt good as he left that day to go home to his wife, Gemme in the apartment they had recently rented on the north side of the Evansville Regional Airport.

Gemme met him at the door. Her brown hair shimmered in the setting sun. A smile didn't wreath her face until Harry let her know how the first day at work went. "Honey, it went great. I accomplished what Mr. Fleming asked of me."

She gave him a hug and a kiss, then she hurriedly exited the room to stir the home-made stew she had simmering on the stove. Harry watched her as she left the room.

About the time they sat down to dinner the dishes did a faint rattle as one of the passenger planes took off from the nearby airport, their very close neighbor. They were trying to get used to the take-offs and landings. After the first spoonful of stew, Harry complimented her, "Honey, this is great stew. Do you have a secret recipe?"

"Yes, I cooked the meat for several hours to make it tender. I'm glad you like it," Gemme commented.

After dishes that night, they sat together on the old couch which they had gotten from Gemme's Aunt May. Harry was enjoying a restful night after the first day as a real attorney not just a student studying law.

The second day Harry was filled to the brim with ambition. Again, Gladys received Harry's cheery greeting. Overnight, Mr. Johnson, the firm's other senior partner, had conferred with Mr. Fleming who had given him a good report on Harry's initial research. Harry hadn't even gotten to the office coffee pot when Mr. Johnson intercepted his journey.

So, Mr. Johnson had two cases and a personal interview on a pro bono case to hand him. Immediately after Harry received the news, he said to himself, "This is going to be a rough day."

To shore up his stamina, he got a huge mug of coffee to accompany him to the research room with its dusty law books stretched to within a foot of the ceiling on all four walls.

First, he perused the two cases to see if there was one easier than the other. Nope, no such luck. Harry took the top one and began his research. After delving into four different laws books, he still hadn't found a precedent suitable. Harry heard a tap-tap on the window. Gladys was notifying him it was break time. He sure could use a break from all the continuous and strenuous concentration he had been doing.

The senior partners didn't join them for coffee, just the hourly workers. Harry quickly struck up a conversation with Gladys. "Boy, I got nowhere this morning."

Gladys chimed in, "Be patient. I know you did some research in college but here there's also a time constraint." Smiling, she added, "Harry, you can do it."

Harry looked directly at Gladys, "Could you do me a favor?"

"Sure, Harry, what do you need?" she asked.

Harry immediately spoke up, "Could you call and set up an

interview with the person in Mr. Johnson's pro bono case? This afternoon or tomorrow will be fine."

"I'll give you the info as soon as I set up your interview. Oh, will you need a notepad for the meeting? If so, I'll get one out of the supply room for you," she volunteered.

Harry graciously replied, "Thanks," as he headed back to the research room. He was going to give it the old college try to get all of Mr. Johnson's requests completed before he left the office.

At lunch, Harry joined office staff as they all went across the street to D. G. Ritzy's fast food restaurant. Harry tried to forget work and join in the light-hearted discussion.

After they ate, Harry was one of the first to ask, "Are we ready to go?" His goal for the day was on his mind.

The office staff finally returned to the office ten minutes early. Harry split off and went straight to work. About four o'clock, he had the two cases done and Gladys had set up the interview he requested for tomorrow at four.

Harry straightened his tired shoulders and took his research to Mr. Johnson. Mr. Johnson laid down what he was reading to check out Harry's research.

"Hmm," Mr. Johnson said several times as he looked over the information. "Harry, good precedent on the first case but the precedent on the second case doesn't quite fit. The case was not quite the same as ours." Then Mr. Johnson looked up into Harry's eyes. "Young man, you've done a good job. I expected you to take several days. You have done a wonderful job in one day. I know you'll work out fine here. Oh, here's the synopsis for the second case." Mr. Johnson breathed deeply a time or two then spoke again. "How about the pro bono case?"

"Sir, I have the interview set up for four tomorrow. Do you have a special aspect I should probe for?"

"No, just search for solid evidence both for and against. We have to be ready for the district attorney's questions. If there is blatant evidence against our client I need to know. Okay?"

"Yes, Sir," Harry answered and exited the room.

That night back home, he bragged to Gemme about how he had accomplished more than Mr. Johnson expected.

The days passed into weeks. By the end of the first month, the senior partners had learned to depend on Harry's rapid and accurate research. They no longer did any of their own research but placed it in the capable hands of their young clerk. Mr. Fleming set up an 'In and Out' tray just for Harry. Daily they had three to five cases to work on so Harry began to have to stay extra hours to get the work done that they had laid on him.

At home, things began to deteriorate. Gemme began to make little remarks about how lonely it was in the apartment on the evenings he worked so late. It was about the time Harry's days at work sometimes were approaching twelve-hour days. He also began to experience headaches. Harry contemplated, "I was a champion athlete in high school and college. Never have I had headaches. I always thought only old folks like mom and dad had these. Oh, well, this could be the price of getting to the top."

One night after Harry finished his usual microwaved warmed-up meal, Gemme sat close to Harry on Aunt May's couch. "Honey, lately you have been working longer hours. After my housework is done, I have almost nothing to do. I am wondering how you would feel if I got a job. We might get an older used car or I could use the bus lines for transportation." She sat silently for several minutes because she had never broached this subject with Harry before. Gemme looked expectantly at him for his answer. She was nervous and was about ready to speak when Harry changed position on the couch and looked intently at her.

"Honey, we don't need the extra money. Mr. Fleming pays me well. But, you brought up the item of being lonely. As I am climbing toward being a full partner, I don't feel I can ask for a lighter load," Harry explained.

Gemme offered an option, "I would be satisfied with a part-time job. That way they wouldn't have to pay my insurance and retirement." She leaned back as if that was all she had to say at that moment.

Harry slowly began to answer her question. "Gemme, I think I understand your situation. I'm busy every minute at the office and have often wished for a moment of relaxation while you wish for something to do. Since you don't have to go to work, I don't feel threatened or intimidated about you going to work. Honey, I think that would be a grand idea. You have my whole-hearted blessing." Then he smiled and leaned over for a hug and maybe a kiss, pleased that they had pleasantly worked out that family problem without raising their voices or arguing.

As the months sped by, the senior partners gained confidence in Harry's research and relinquished all the background work for all their cases to Him. Before Harry came on board, Mr. Fleming and Mr. Johnson did their own research to make sure it was done right. Harry's In-tray was growing larger and larger. Many times, the cases had time constraints and were more involved. The senior partners didn't mind paying Harry overtime. That extra time gave them leisure to take their families out to the Country Club for more evening meals together. Neither partner ever commented on all the extra hours Harry was working. For them it was finally a lighter workload on them and a perk of being a senior partner in the firm.

Late one Thursday afternoon, Mr. Johnson poked his head into the research room and in a low voice said, "Harry, I'd like to see you in my office."

Inside his head, Harry said, "Oh, no." Harry remembered the time he was called to the principal's office over the school intercom. This sinking feeling felt much like that. So, Harry slowly arose and marked his place in this research and headed in the direction of Mr. Johnson's office.

"Come in and close the door. Have seat!" Mr. Johnson commanded.

Harry gently sat down and was ready for whatever was coming.

Mr. Johnson's face had a stern look on it, so he wasn't going to be praised, Harry assured himself. "I'm a lawyer and I need to be brave and take what's coming, like a true lawyer," he told himself.

Mr. Johnson plowed right into his speech. "This afternoon I was thoroughly embarrassed. I have not had that feeling since my first case as a young lawyer. I almost shriveled up and slid under my table. That is the most uncomfortable I have ever felt. Do you know why?"

The office staff may have known something was up because Harry always stayed in his room. Harry could have given a smart-aleck answer, but he meekly replied, "No, I don't have the faintest idea."

"Today the District Attorney surprised me with some simple but damaging evidence. I got shot down. It ruined my whole defense. In your interview with our pro bono client, you didn't probe hard enough for the facts. Our client did not disclose all the facts. She owned a gun and she did fire it. So, Harry don't let that happen again. Dig deep for evidence for us **but** also for the evidence the District Attorney can use against us so we won't lose the case or be so embarrassed again," Mr. Johnson sternly gave the order.

Contritely, Harry replied, "Sir, I'll be more thorough and careful in my interviews and research. I promise to cover the whole case so our lawyers won't look like beginners, or our firm appear inept. Again, I'm very sorry."

Mr. Johnson gruffly growled, "You may go."

The whole office staff was looking at Harry and his expression as he exited Mr. Johnson's office. They all had heard Mr. Johnson raise his voice although they couldn't understand what was said. They saw Harry trudge over to the research room like a whipped puppy.

That night Harry left the office two minutes after five. Gladys said, "Harry, we'll be thinking about you tonight.

Tomorrow will be better." The door closed behind him on the worst day of his career.

Gemme was surprised that he beat her home from her job she had recently taken as bookkeeper at a nearby adult care center. Harry was not hungry but Gemme fixed a soothing cup of hot tea with honey in it. Just after she handed it to him, she carefully sat next to him and patiently waited for him to tell her what happened at work.

"Honey, I let Mr. Johnson down and he let me know it. We were in his office with the door shut, when he told me that I hadn't carefully gotten all the evidence from his client. The District Attorney brought out evidence I didn't unearth, and we lost the case hands down and Mr. Johnson felt thoroughly embarrassed." Then Harry leaned back on the couch waiting for Gemme to add to his misery.

"Oh, Babe, I feel so sorry for you. You know that I love you. This was a rough situation, but I know that this is a lesson you will never forget." She laid her arm over his shoulder and consoled him.

***

As Harry began his third year with the firm, the two senior partners evaluated Harry's progress. Mr. Fleming commented that Harry's research was always rapid, thorough and accurate. Mr. Johnson brought up the fact that after he reprimanded Harry for not getting all the evidence for a case, he was an excellent worker. Harry was proud he had not repeated every word Mr. Johnson had said to the office staff. Although Mr.

Johnson had consistently loaded Harry down, he admired his work ethic. The consensus was he was very prepared to do lawyer-type work now. He had proven himself worthy of more important work.

The firm hired a young paralegal named Alice to do the research work on cases. Harry began showing her some of the strategies involved in locating the appropriate precedents she would need.

The following Monday Mr. Fleming called him into the office. "Harry, I'm proud of you. Mr. Johnson and I have come to rely on your research. We feel you are ready to work on supposedly easy cases, pro bono cases and out of court cases to get your feet wet. This means you'll have these cases all on your own. For you, they will be sink or swim cases. Today, you can have the rest of the day off and to go to Roberts Stadium to see a ball game or take your wife out to a luxurious dinner. Tomorrow, we'll have a docket of cases for you to start on."

Harry stood up and said, "Thank you for your confidence. I'll work hard to prove worthy of it," as he turned and headed for the front door.

"Hey, Harry! Wait a minute. Could you come back for a minute?" Mr. Fleming yelled. Gladys looked up to take it all in. Mr. Fleming never shouted.

Harry turned around and retraced his steps, He looked up into Mr. Fleming smiling face. Harry thought, "This is not like the last time I got yelled at."

Mr. Fleming's face straightened up as he looked directly at Harry. "I was thinking. I suggested you take Gemme out to dinner. Our firm has a membership at the Evansville Country Club. Let me call and set up a dinner appointment for two at 7:30 this evening using our membership." Then he paused for Harry to answer.

"Could you do that for us? If Gemme is strongly against it, I can call and cancel. But … I can't imagine her turning that down," Harry replied. Then he headed for the front door with a lively step. Gladys whispered as he passed her desk, "You and Gemme enjoy a night out."

When Harry got home, he called Gemme at her adult care center. "Honey, could you ask off early tonight? I'm home and everything is fine. Mr. Fleming gave me the rest of the day off," smilingly, he continued, "for good behavior."

"Okay I'll do that and call you back." Seconds later, she called back and informed Harry she'd be home about three o'clock.

No sooner had she entered the door of the apartment Harry said, "Gemme, let's do something special with our evening, if you aren't too tired."

With the possibility of a night out with her sweetheart all her tiredness instantly evaporated, and a new vitality invaded her body. "Harry, what did you have to mind?"

"Well, Mr. Fleming gave me a couple of suggestions as I hurried out of the office. A ball game at Robert's Stadium or a nice dinner at the Evansville Country Club."

Gemme quickly replied, "I'll take the nice dinner out. But I'm not sure I have the right kind of clothes to wear."

"It's settled then. We'll go out for dinner. I'll let you search for an outfit and I'll see if my tuxedo still fits around the waist," Harry concluded as they went their separate ways, ready to explore their closets.

Harry got his cell phone out and found a flower shop to deliver a corsage to the house in the next hour. With that settled, he joined Gemme in the bedroom.

Gemme couldn't find the fancy dress that she thought she packed when they moved. But she did find a halter dress she hadn't worn in a while. She slipped it on. It fit! It was her favorite color, royal blue. It was a long dress. Also, out of the bottom drawer of a dresser, she pulled a complimentary ivory colored shawl to go with it.

Harry whispering aloud said, "Now I just have to find something to wear," and raising his voice to a louder call, "Honey, did you pack my tuxedo?" Harry asked.

"No, Babe, I thought you had outgrown that besides we didn't have room, but you have a nice black suit and a grey one, either of which would be just right."

"Thanks, Honey. I found the black one," just as the doorbell rang. "I'll get it," he said as he paid for the flowers and placed them on the table next to the front door.

They didn't get a limo but Gemme was just glad to spend time with her sweet husband. They left their car at the Club entrance with the valet and walked in. Her stride showed class. Everyone saw the slim fitting blue dress and the ivory shawl graciously draped over her shoulders. Occasionally, her low-heeled sandals peeked out from under the long dress. The club employees checked out the wife of the new attorney from the Fleming & Johnson Law Firm.

Gemme and Harry enjoyed the meal and had one dance in the middle of the room. Two older couples joined them to make it complete. After the dance, one of the couples introduced themselves as Mr. Justin and Kadie Jones. Harry informed them he was part of the Fleming & Johnson Law Firm.

On the way home Gemme said, "Honey, that was a wonderful evening I'll never forget. Thank you."

Back at work the next morning, true to his word, Mr. Fleming had a half dozen cases stacked on a desk in the office area with an official nameplate that read, "Atty Harry McKenzie". Harry was appreciative that the firm recognized all his years of schooling and the last three years of his work for the firm.

Before he sat down to his own desk, he went to the company coffee pot. There he met Gladys. "Isn't that nice? My own desk," he commented.

"A couple weeks ago, Mr. Fleming had me order your name plate. I saw them moving in your desk yesterday. I'm so glad for you." Cautiously she continued, "Harry, it may mean even more work."

With a new vigor, he put his finger in the ear of the mug and twirled around and headed to **his** own desk. Carefully, he lifted the stack of cases and began to choose which one to start on first. What a delight to not be stuck in the research room with no windows all by himself, but out here with the office traffic. On top of that it also meant a raise in pay and a raise in status.

Harry picked a case. It was a car accident; the client was

suing for $500,000 in damages which included replacement of an SUV and medical expenses for damage to her spinal column.

He got on the phone and set up an appointment with the client for that afternoon. Then he sifted through the others. The most appealing was an airplane crash. Someone was suing an aircraft company. This would take a precise precedent to sue the corporation with their team of seasoned attorneys. So, the rest of the morning he joined Alice in the research room. This kind of felt comfortable because he had spent three long years in here. He and Alice hardly spoke but it felt like they were comrades working side by side. Before the plane accident case interview, Harry had found a precedent, but it didn't quite fit. It seemed weak plus the corporation could win with that precedent. Somewhere in the research room was the right one. He just had to find it.

The lady involved in the car accident suit came in and Gladys introduced her to Harry. She was middle-aged, rather plump, but was not haughty or aggressive. "Good afternoon, Mrs. Flahardy. Please have a seat here next to my desk. That way the rest of the office won't hear us address confidential material. My number one need to help you win your case is the whole truth. We need every feeling or intuition you have, if you can put them into words. I must have what you think is a good part of your case, as well as what you think might keep you from winning your case. Okay?" Harry concluded.

"I understand," she said.

"May I record this on my phone? My secretary will transcribe it. That way I won't miss one fact or one feeling."

"That's fine, Mr. McKenzie," she okayed.

So for the next two hours Harry asked questions trying to get every detail involved in the accident.

Mrs. Flahardy did a good job, but her shoulders looked slumped as she exited the building and it was evident that she was exhausted and in some pain.

The next morning, he found the precise precedent for the car accident. By now, Gladys had the interview typed so Harry spent the rest of the day looking over the transcript for the good and bad points of the case. Two thirds of the interview was pertinent and useful in winning the case and was material he could use in preparing the brief he would send to the judge.

2

First Home

> Success is when I add value to myself.
> Significance is when I add value to others."
>
> **~ John C. Maxwell**

Harry got the idea they needed a home to match his new promotion. "I'll discuss this with my sweet wife tonight. I'll just wait until after dinner, maybe during dessert," he thought. But, no sooner had he opened the door he yelled, "Gemme?"

From the kitchen a girlish voice called, "I'm in here."

Harry immediately headed that way. He just couldn't wait. "Honey, I've got an idea."

Gemme turned off the burner on the stove and intently looked into Harry's eyes. "What's your idea?" she quizzed.

"Let's sit here at the kitchen table and we can discuss it," suggested Harry.

Gemme was feeling good as she daintily sat in the kitchen

chair and patiently waited for him to start the conversation, drawn-out or in rapid fire.

"Since I moved out of the research room and into the common area with my own desk and my own name plate and the $10,000 a year raise," Harry began but Gemme interrupted him.

"That's nice, huh? You must feel so good by no longer being a clerk. They kept you there at least a year longer than any other law firm. It's about time," Gemme firmly stated.

Gemme quickly rose from the chair holding out her arms for a hug. "Honey, that is so good. I'm really proud of your advancement. They are going to treat you like the attorney you are."

After a long loving congratulatory hug, Gemme let the news soak in. It was now a reality that Harry, her sweet husband, was finally achieving his life-time goal.

Harry sat down again in the chair so Gemme took for granted the news was all delivered. As she went back toward the stove to finish dinner, he began again to further explain his idea. "On the way home I was thinking about purchasing our own home," then he fell silent waiting for her input.

"Babe, I'm accustomed to our apartment, but I understand that you're thinking about what a true lawyer should have. I won't hold you back. Do you have a time frame in mind?" she asked.

Harry leaned against the back of his chair and took a breath and then exhaled. In an even tone, like a confident lawyer starting his summation he said, "I thought we could search the

Evansville Courier this week and maybe Saturday look at some properties," Harry questioningly projected.

Her voice was pitched a little higher than usual at such an immediate action. "Oh … that's pretty quick, but I'm with you. I'll let my mind work it," she said. Shortly thereafter, Gemme was mentally picturing boxes and sorting and all the other details that would be necessary. By the end of the week Gemme had circled several homes in the *Evansville Courier* for consideration.

From their apartment close to the Evansville Regional Airport they drove through downtown and headed west to near Southern Indiana University and then turned south. It was the area at the edge of the business district which meant all the fast food restaurants would be close by.

On Irvington Avenue, they spotted a nice, well-kept house. The full-length front porch was brick while the rest was a frame building with white vinyl siding. "Harry, this one is priced at $149,900," she said, "it resembles my folks' home."

Harry continued, "We are so close to the university that we'll probably be interrupted by the loud band music, yelling pep rallies and very heavy traffic on football game nights." That shut down the discussion on that property. "Honey, what is next house you have circled in the *Courier*?" he asked.

Gemme refolded the paper to the middle column and went to the next red circle. "We need to go toward Newburgh to Pine Break Drive." He turned right on the Lloyd Expressway to quickly get across town. The designated house was a red brick, ranch-style home. It was situated on a spacious raised plot of land but the neighborhood lawns and shrubs were't neat or trimmed. One house was in disrepair and the houses needed paint. Harry voiced his opinion quickly, "With neighborhood lawns like this, it looks like people just don't care."

"Harry, you didn't even ask the sale price. It is only $169,900," she explained.

"I know, but the surroundings turn me off. What is the address of the next one?" Harry quizzed, anxious to move on to the next location.

Gemme quickly replied, "It is Saybrook Drive. That's north on Route 41, a little past the airport."

As they turned off the four-lane highway, they instantly saw better maintained homes with manicured lawns and trimmed hedges. Several had long driveways. A few were gravel, some were blacktop, but most were concrete.

"Gemme, I'm liking this already. What is the house number?"

"Babe, that is it on your left." Harry pulled just into that driveway and stopped. They were looking at a palatial brick house with a double car garage and three gables looking at them.

"Honey, what is the sale price on this beautiful house?" he asked with anticipation.

"Well ...," Gemme slowly started, "It is 3,000 square feet, two bathrooms and three bedrooms ..."

Harry interrupted, "Get to the price, please."

"They are asking $315,000. Sorry," she apologized. "I got caught up in the description of all the rooms."

Without making any more observations, he announced in

a rather strong voice, "This is a suitable sized home for an attorney from Fleming & Johnson Law Firm to own and soon to be Fleming, Johnson and McKenzie Law Firm."

The next evening, they scheduled an inspection with the realtor. Gemme was as pleased with the inside as Harry was with the size of the house and the surrounding neighborhood.

Since they had a good credit rating, they made arrangements to purchase the house and the loan went right through. Harry was able to make a $34,000 down payment and kept the monthly payment less than $2500 a month which was easy to handle with his new raise.

They gave a move notice at the apartment office and booked an Allied Moving Van. It was easy to schedule the movers since their district office was just two miles south on Route 41.

The heavy load of work on the cases seemed to keep pouring into his file for the next whole year. It was only a few nights that he had to work only a couple of hours overtime. When he had to work late, Harry was always courteous and called Gemme and notified her.

While on morning coffee break, Mr. Johnson stepped out of his secluded office and nodded for Harry to come in. So, Harry stuck his finger in the cup handle and went to see what Mr. Johnson wanted. It was seldom if ever good.

"Harry," Mr. Johnson greeted him after he stepped over the threshold. "I have a simple document I need typed. I'd do it, but I have a case in court in an hour. When you get done, could you bring it over to the courthouse? I know you'll have to drive your own car because it's at least three miles away. Oh, before

I forget it, it must be error-free. The document is a conveyance of property for my client. I need it before the judge pronounces the verdict."

Harry immediately left Mr. Johnson's office. On the way back to his desk, Harry gave his mug a lift to Gladys indicating everything was okay.

First, Harry brought up the form on the computer. Then he looked over the notes Mr. Johnson had given him examining it for the cost of the property and the exact names while Mr. Johnson rushed out of the office to get over to the courthouse on time.

Harry wasn't sure of Mr. Johnson's handwritten i's and e's. So, he went over to Mr. Johnson's office in hopes he could find some document with their exact names typed out. Harry felt uneasy as he entered the private territory of Mr. Johnson while he was not there. He felt like everyone in the office was watching him. The third place Harry looked, he found what he needed, so without messing up or changing the order of any paperwork on Mr. Johnson's desk. Then he promptly left.

Quickly he got back to work. Harry theorized Glady could have done these three times faster, but a lawyer really ought to do it. "I guess that is why he asked me to prepare this conveyance of property document," Harry reasoned.

It was a full half hour later when he stood near the main office printer and stapled the sheets together and labeled a blue manila folder and placed the document in it.

As he hurried by Gladys he said, "I'm delivering this to Mr. Johnson over at the courthouse." The front door banged behind him. No sooner had he gotten down the road, Harry got blocked by an accident and traffic was alternating around the tow truck. "I'm going to be late and then Mr. Johnson will have another thing to be mean to me about."

Finally, he got around the accident and went faster than the speed limit to the courthouse. He slammed the car door and ran to the front door and bounded up the steps to the main courtroom. After telling the officer who was guarding outside the door who he was and that he had information regarding the case in session the guard slowly opened the huge door.

Walking on the balls of his feet, he very quietly headed for Mr. Johnson. Harry happened to glance up at the judge who was giving him a disapproving stare. When Mr. Johnson heard him coming, he smiled and mouthed a thank you. Harry found the closest empty seat and parked. He took in the surroundings. Even though he had studied law and worked for a law firm for several years, he had not yet experienced handling a case by himself in court.

After the case adjourned, Mr. Johnson actually said in words, "Harry, thanks. You made it in time," then he went back to his business.

Harry headed out to his car. As he strode across the parking lot, he thought, "I'm glad it wasn't me in that accident and missed getting the document at all to Mr. Johnson. He could feel the tension slowly leave his neck and shoulders.

3

First Trial

> "Have a clear vision of your future and take action every day to move towards it. You deserve it."
>
> **~ Damien Thomas**

A few months after the move into the common area Mr. Fleming sauntered over to Harry's desk carrying a large case file. "Harry, I have an interesting case for you. It is time to try your wings with your first case. Your client is presently out on bail. The defendant, our client wants a jury trial. His name is Greg and has been accused of beating up one brother, Shev, and causing over $10,000 damage, essentially totaling the car of his older brother, Shawn. Our client claims he's innocent and was never near that brother's car the night this was supposed to have happened. Greg's only witness is his girlfriend, Barbara, who says they were together until 10:30 then Greg says he went home and was alone until he left for work the next morning. All their statements have been taken under oath. The trial is scheduled in 30 days. You have lots of work ahead in the next three short weeks. The assistant DA, Diane Carr, is prosecuting. I believe you will do our firm proud." He added, "I guess my advice to you is to keep a close check on your jury's reactions, especially as you present your evidence. The other piece of advice I usually give is do adequate research, but I've seen you do that excellently."

Mr. Fleming tried to use the excuse for giving Harry the case so late. He said his schedule was so heavy he just wouldn't be able to handle it.

Harry took the case file from him, trying to keep his hands steady and display a look of confidence. It was very short notice but he assured Mr. Fleming he would do his best.

After Mr. Fleming was completely back in his office, Harry slowly made his way over to Gladys' desk and with a big smile whispered, "I have my first solo case before a judge and jury."

As usual she was glad to hear the good news and encouragingly told him, "I know you can do it. I'm sure you'll be well prepared. I'm proud of you, Harry. If there is anything at all I can help you with, please feel free to ask."

Next, from his desk he called Gemme on his iPhone and told her about the new assignment. Gemme promptly replied, "Honey, I've been waiting for this for you a long time. Let's go out for dinner tonight and celebrate, then you can buckle down and get your defense lined out. You need to enjoy and celebrate this opportunity." They did go out to a nice restaurant and enjoyed the meal and relaxed with the smooth music in the background but trying his first case seemed to occupy his thoughts most of the evening. He was beginning to feel the pressure.

The first thing Harry did to begin in preparation for his case was to meet with Greg separately and then with him and his girlfriend, Barbara. Greg said, "The only dealings I've had with either of my brothers are occasionally at the auto store where I work. They have never been really friendly, but lately have been almost antagonistic toward me. I had a couple of phone calls from our sister, Sheryl, though asking me to meet with her."

Barbara, Greg's girlfriend swore she didn't know the brothers but had dealings with their sister on a couple of occasions. "One was when I caught her shoplifting and another time, I caught her breaking into a package of makeup and removing some contents at the drugstore where I work."

Harry questioned, "Did you call the police or report her to your boss?

"No," Barbara relied, "but I gave her a verbal warning both times, hoping that would be enough. She appeared to be very embarrassed."

Harry began thinking the sister, Sheryl, might have initiated the accusations but all statements were under oath and physical injury to Shev and property damage to Shawn's car had been documented.

Harry lined up character witnesses for Greg with Glady's help. He feared he would lose the case due to the fact there were sworn statements of the accusers.

Only a few days before the court date, Harry was having difficulty sleeping. There were a couple of details yet to work out, so rather than toss and turn in bed and keep Gemme awake he decided to go into the office even though it was not yet six o'clock. That morning when Harry walked in to work on the case, he couldn't find it. He searched in all the drawers in his desk. The file was nowhere in the office. He tried to concentrate on the search until Gladys came in at 7:30.

"Harry, your face is all tense. What's the matter?" she inquired, looking at him with concern as she unlocked her desk. Obviously, something was wrong.

"Well, I am missing my file for Greg's court case. Have you seen it anywhere? I have searched everywhere including the research room. I'm not that careless to leave it lying around. My stomach is rolling. I can't afford to start over," he explained trying to stay calm. He could feel a headache growing behind his eyes.

"Let me look around and then you can check with Mr. Fleming or Mr. Johnson when they come in, okay?" she suggested. After checking, she was also unsuccessful. "Okay, Harry I guess it is time to check the senior partners."

So, he nervously arose and headed for Mr. Fleming's office as soon as he arrived and gave a light rap on the door frame. He looked in just as Mr. Fleming was raising his head. Harry asked, "Mr. Fleming, have you seen my case file laying around? I can't seem to find it."

Without any interest, he replied, "No, I can't imagine where it might be," and immediately turned back to his desk leaving Harry standing in the doorway."

"Thanks, I'll keep looking," Harry replied under his breath

then turned and headed toward the coffee pot. He made a sharp turn toward Mr. Johnson's office and rapped lightly on his door frame. He had to find that file. Weeks of work were in that folder. At this point, Harry was not feeling optimistic and very nervous.

"Come in," Mr. Johnson replied as he reshuffled a pile of papers on his desk.

Harry timidly stepped into the room. "Mr. Johnson, I can't find my Hardy Family case file and I wondered if you'd seen it? Last I saw it, it was in the lower left drawer of my desk."

Mr. Johnson seemed caught by surprise but quickly slipped his hand to the upper left-hand corner of his desk and grabbed the file. He looked almost embarrassed when he handed it to Harry. "Well … I had a minute last night to look it over and see how prepared you were. I thought as a senior partner I should check since this was your first case. I really should have placed it back where I found it. And, yes it looks like you are doing well. Good luck on your preparations and the case in court," he told Harry. Then, Mr. Johnson settled back in his chair and began to reminisce about his own son, Roger, and wondered how he was doing. "If I had a wish I would like him to be like Harry. Its been a long time since I've had any contact with him…I think its been over five years this Thanksgiving." He missed him each and every day.

Harry thanked Mr. Johnson and tried to minimize the irritation with the intrusion into his case without his permission. He walked out of the room. Harry was very annoyed and his stress level was at maximum. Once at this desk, he tried to concentrate with some deep breathing. Suddenly he realized he felt very tired and the day had barely begun.

Harry continued his preparation by visualizing his appearance and conduct before the jury picturing himself with a look of confidence and not appearing like this was his first case. Subsequently, he worked on his opening statement of laying out his case, and what his aim was and what he hoped would be the jury's decision. As the trial drew closer, he wrote down his summation that would come before the judge handed the case over to the jury. He would develop and present his case as perfectly as he could. There would be no room for error. Harry definitely felt the tension building each day.

The court date finally arrived. Early that morning, Harry took a hot shower, put on his favorite white shirt without one wrinkle, his good grey suit and added a bold red and grey striped tie. The trip to the office to pick up all his notes and attaché case were routine. But …, the routine stopped as he headed up the front steps of the courthouse. "Harry," he whispered to himself, "be confident. Don't let any of your fear be seen." Immediately, Harry imperceptibly threw his shoulders back and took in a large deep breath on each of the next three steps.

Harry met up with Greg outside the courtroom and looked him over to make sure he was presentable. Harry had previously coached him to only answer the questions, not to elaborate. Harry was confident they had covered all bases. Then they entered the bustling courtroom together. Harry wasn't very relaxed because he felt his shoes hit the floor every step the entire way to the designated table in front of the judge.

When Harry and the DA were in place, the judge's name was announced, the gavel sounded, and the jury selection commenced. There was one person Harry turned down because they were super keen on finding someone guilty. The DA excluded two others because of prejudice against punishment. All in all, Harry felt good about the selected jurists.

After the DA slammed Harry's client with accusations, it was Harry's turn. He left his notes and stood, adjusted his tie and went to a spot in front of the 12 members of the jury. His first three sentences were tremulous, but he quickly evened out. It was the jitters similar to what he remembered with his first few pitches in the state baseball championship back in high school. Within a few moments he began to relax, and his words flowed professionally and confidently.

He only left out one small point from his prepared notes, then sat down next to his client. Harry tried not to show it but let out a long slow breath. Quickly, he mentally reviewed what he had done so far. Today he was learning that a person can be giving information yet comprehending other's receptiveness at the same time. During his opening, the jury's expressions were fairly stoic except for one lady on the left end of the second row who seemed to hang on every word. He couldn't tell whether she would be the holdout on a decision or possibly be the convincer for his case.

Diana Carr, the assistant DA was giving her presentations with more gestures and animations but that didn't seem to make her more effective according to the faces of the jury. She called her witnesses and when the sister was called, the jury saw Sheryl tear up. The Assistant DA was cross examining the details of the brother's injury and the car damage she reported witnessing. Then she actually began to cry. The Assistant DA called for a trial recess.

Back in the courtroom the brothers repeated their stories, then admitted to accusing Greg just to get even for their sister. Greg had been leaving her out of family functions. The second reason was Barbara, Greg's girlfriend, for embarrassing her in the store when she caught her shoplifting. It was a very emotional situation for everyone involved.

The jury was dismissed, and all charges were dropped against Greg and the brothers were ordered to pay all court fees. Greg did not press charges. He felt his two brothers had put themselves and their sister through enough shame, fraud and deception.

As soon as Harry got to the car, he called Gemme and gave her the news of his victory. "Honey, if you would like to celebrate, and get a nice new dress, I would make reservations at the Evansville Country Club."

After she caught her breath, Gemme told him, "I think I'd like to fix you a fine dinner right here at home and the two of us enjoy a relaxing evening together."

"Oh, Gemme, that's a wonderful idea. Thank you, I am very tired," he told her trying to shrug off the tension in his neck and back.

"I'll look for you later this afternoon, and I'm so glad it went well for you," she complimented. She was looking forward to hearing the details if he'd share them.

4

True Crisis

> "Our words reveal our heart. Our
> actions reveal our soul."
>
> ~ **Anthony D. Williams**

This Friday was special. Harry gave Gladys his usual cheerful greeting as the front door slammed behind him. He glanced at the In-box on his desk and wasn't very upset because he only saw one new folder. Harry kept his stride as he continued his trip toward the office coffee pot, appreciative that Gladys always came in early and prepared the big 30-cup coffee pot for the office staff. After he poured the steaming coffee into his favorite mug, he headed toward his desk lifted his mug slightly, so Gladys could see his signal of thanks.

After he was seated, he slowly drank three long slow swallows. He sized up his day. Harry had a case almost ready to close and the one he researched unsuccessfully for a precedent yesterday, plus the new folder! That was normal so why in the world did it seem like a mountain of work? He checked his overall feelings. "I feel draggy this morning. Come to think of it I had trouble choosing a suit plus my hot shower didn't lift my spirits as it usually does," Harry concluded. Something just felt off.

Harry leaned back in his wide-armed wooden swivel chair. He hadn't graduated to the high back, overstuffed leather chairs yet. As he had another drink of rather lukewarm coffee, he told himself, "I guess I better get this work done no matter how I feel. Another thing is I'm a lot younger than Mr. Fleming and Mr. Johnson why am I feeling so worn out? Self! Straighten up – body, act like the attorney you are," he told himself. He sluggishly picked up the almost completed case and began carefully examining it for errors and possible loopholes that the Assistant District Attorney might use against him. His body seemed to respond a little to the mental pep-talk he gave it though he still felt lightheaded.

Just after he returned to his desk after morning break, he felt a heavy, aching pain going down his left arm. He tried to shake it out like he used to do as a baseball pitcher. That didn't help. It was only a short time later it began to feel like a blacksmith had placed a heavy anvil on his chest. He also found it difficult to take a normal breath. He noticed he'd begun to perspire heavily.

"Gladys!" Harry softly shouted. She quickly came over and could see he was in pain and having trouble getting his breath. Even his color had changed from when he'd come in that morning. He was looking very pale.

"Harry, I'm going to call 911," she assured him as she picked up his phone. "Try to relax as much as you can," she said as she stayed by his side.

Harry tried to relax, but the pain was becoming severe. It seemed only minutes when the front doors swung open with two EMT's and a rolling gurney. Gladys was still at Harry's desk and had helped him loosen his tie and shirt collar.

The lead EMT began to ask questions. "Where do you hurt? How severe?" The EMT noticed his lips had a bluish cast and ordered the second EMT to get an oxygen canister from under the gurney and plastic oxygen line. The tubing was quickly placed under his nose and looped over his ears. Harry didn't feel like it helped much because all he could think of was this pain and heaviness in his chest and shortness of breath. The lead EMT put a clip on this index finger to register his oxygen level.

The lead EMT looked over to his assistant and in a calm voice said, "Call ahead and give them our ETA. Let's get him on the gurney and get him to St. Mary's Hospital quickly." Moments later the gurney was in high gear and the three were headed for the front door. Only moments later Gladys heard the siren start wailing.

Everyone in the office began interrogating Gladys. One worker exclaimed, "How could that happen in our office?" The senior partners came out of their offices just as the front door slammed and they listened as Gladys explained about Harry's possible heart attack. Very slowly the office staff went back to work one at a time. They were concerned not only for Harry but with the thought that it could have been them. Before Gladys went back to her desk, she traveled over to Mr. Fleming's office door and asked, "They are taking him to St. Mary's. Do you want me to call his wife or are you going to take care of that?"

Mr. Fleming firmly stated, "I'm going to call her right now so she'll be able to meet the ambulance. Thank you, Gladys, for being there with him. Let's all pray he's going to be all right."

Harry laid there as the ambulance bounced along. He kept wondering if he was going to die. He heard the siren shut off as they entered the hospital driveway. They rolled him out of the ambulance and clicked the wheels down. Soon, he saw light fixture after light fixture whiz by overhead. The EMT's backed him into an exam room in the ER.

The nurse in charge was most concerned about Harry's oxygen level as she transferred the oxygen tube from the portable to the hospital supply and connected the pulse oximeter on Harry's finger to give an accurate reading of his oxygen level.

A resident doctor soon entered the room, studied the info on the EMT's chart then walked the couple of steps over to Harry. "Your symptoms indicate you may be having a heart attack. The nurse will bring you a form to sign that we'll need to draw some blood, do some further testing and take some pictures to determine if there is coronary blockage before further damage is done to your heart. If we find blockage, the form will give us permission to quickly get to that blockage before irreversible damage occurs to your heart muscle."

Harry nodded, yes, and signed the form. Things began to move quickly from that moment on. The nurse had helped Harry out of his street clothes and into a gown just as Gemme pulled back the curtain to see her hubby.

The head nurse tentatively scheduled the operating room in case the imaging showed a single or multiple blockage. The cardiac team was put on preliminary alert for a possible angioplasty.

The specialist who viewed the results spotted two arteries that were completely blocked. The doctors decided on an angioplasty and called on the Cardiac team. Within 30 minutes, they had Harry prepped for the procedure.

During the procedure, Gemme waited nervously and checked often with the receptionist. She had a small 10-oz Pepsi from the vending machine and tried valiantly to relax. It was impossible. In the quiet, she recalled recently noticing slight changes in his behavior and his overall tiredness and increased tension.

It was a long hour later when the doctor finally appeared and called for Mrs. McKenzie. Softly the doctor said, "Well, he had a double blockage in the arteries. We got to them and inserted two stents before much damage was done to the heart muscle. He is so fortunate he came in so quickly. Later, when he's out of recovery I'll be by his room and we three will discuss his condition. Any questions?"

"Not at this time. Will he be okay?" Gemme quizzed, near tears.

"If he takes care of himself from here on, he has a great chance at a normal life," the doctor commented and exited seemingly in a rush to go on with a very demanding schedule.

Gemme got to visit Harry in the recovery room, but since Harry was still heavily sedated, she kissed his forehead and left.

The next day Gemme got permission for the day off from her job and came to spend the whole day with him. During morning rounds the doctor stopped in. The doctor quizzed, "Mrs. McKenzie?"

"Yes, Sir. Do you have time now to talk about our case?" Gemme inquired.

As he pulled up the extra chair, Harry rolled his head so they could be facing one another. The doctor looked directly at Harry, but talked loud enough for Gemme to take it all in. "Harry, as I told your wife earlier, since you came in quickly, we got to the blockages and kept the heart muscle from further damage. It's up to you. Since you have no family history of heart disease and you are only 45 years old, you have a better than average chance at a normal healthy life." He continued. "The greatest contributing factors to your having this heart attack were your diet and your stress. Your diet has contributed to fatty deposits in your arteries most likely formed by high cholesterol foods and unbalanced meals. The stress raised your blood pressure. Your long hours contributed to it, too. Your job involves a lot of sitting, right?" he asked looking directly at Harry.

"Yes, sir, I guess I neglected to exercise," Harry confessed, thinking about the long hours and complete exhaustion at the end of those long days.

The doctor began to change his talk to the positive. "Harry, I have a three-point plan. I call it the D-E-E plan. The "D" is for diet." Then the doctor split his attention to include Gemme. "There should be large portions of vegetables on your plate plus fruit with each meal or between meals each day. We prefer the main course be chicken or fish or beans to provide protein." Then the doctor paused, but received no comments from Harry or Gemme, so he plowed on.

"Next is "E" is for emotions. Harry how has your stress level been at work?"

Harry kind of blushed, "I have been putting in twelve hours many days and sometimes sixteen hours at the office to get assignments done on time." Harry stopped abruptly at the confession he had just made.

The doctor looked over at Gemme, "I bet you missed him a lot, right?" the doctor questioned, and smiled when Gemme nodded in agreement.

Then the doctor continued, covering a lot of information in a short time. "The second 'E' is for exercise. Your body definitely needs exercise because it was not created for inactivity. We, in the health field, recommend thirty minutes of continuous exercise daily. That can be aerobics, walking a mile, swimming, or cycling. Many don't have sufficient self-discipline to consistently do aerobics, so I usually try to get a commitment to walk every day." Then he stood up straight like that was the end of the consultation. And, sure enough, it was. The doctor left them but turned around at the door and said, "I'll let you two discuss and decide what you can do together to live a healthier lifestyle."

Harry was due to be released from the hospital the next morning, but when the nurses reported a slightly elevated temperature, the doctor ordered him to stay another day. With Gemme back at work, Harry had a whole day to himself with nothing to do but sit around. So, about seven thirty that morning he began to review his life. "One of my goals was to be a senior partner in the law firm. Up to this point, I have paid my dues. Where has it gotten me so far?" Harry paused a few moments to ponder. "I have put on weight, strained my marriage and wound up with a heart attack. Besides all this, I tried climbing the elusive corporate ladder, worried about pleasing people I didn't care about, reached for goals that really weren't important, cared about getting the latest vehicle and electronic gadgets, and was forced to deal with people who lied, cheated and stole."

Just before his lunch tray was delivered, he was beginning to think that the area of law may not be the best life to give him fulfillment. Again, he thought, "But ... the law field would give me status in the community and sufficient wealth to live in style, but is that what I really want?" Later, he would get together with Gemme and further refine his thoughts. She needed to have input into any decisions that would be made. He knew he certainly didn't want the risk repeating what he'd gone through health wise. The next heart attack might be fatal.

Having to remain in the hospital until his temperature stayed in the normal range for 24 hours gave Harry lots of time to think. As he continued to muse in the quiet of his hospital room, Harry got to reliving his time at the firm. It was day after day for years that Harry's in-box was stacked with many cases which Mr. Fleming or Mr. Johnson viewed as boring or beneath their status. Harry's only solo cases were the routine or civil cases over wills and petty disputes that were always handled out of court. Harry usually presented his cases in a courthouse room with his client and the judge.

From what Harry could tell, he was handling the same number of cases as both the Senior Partners together. It was unending, year after year. Never did they spend any overtime but had time for the gym in the mornings or taking their spouse to the Country Club in the evening while Harry was still in the office working hard. Many cases had a time constraint, so he worked late into the evening and sometimes into the night. Harry did the work he was assigned so he could be a good lawyer. Often, he was so tired he didn't even feel like eating even if Gemme had something nice fixed for him. He was also too tired to go out even if Gemme asked Harry to take her out to G. D. Ritzy's or Grandy's or even McDonald's. Gemme seemed to be bearing up with his tiredness. Frequently, she would ask when he would become Senior Partner. Lately, Gemme had to have antacid tablets handy to help calm his stomach so he could get to sleep. Working at the adult care center seemed to help her tolerate his absence because she wasn't getting much attention or support from him. It saddened Harry not to be able to give Gemme the attention she deserved. Harry recalled how on evenings after work they used to have pleasurable talks about the events of their days. Oh, how wonderful that was! How long ago that seemed.

That evening Harry again reminisced. This extra-long day before release was a genuine time to reflect and appraise his whole life. Now, Harry assessed his inmost feelings.

This was the first time he could remember that he had

relaxed. Just then another thought came up. The morning before his heart attack, Mr. Johnson had walked out of his office over to his desk in front of everyone in the office.

"Here is a rush order. The plaintiff will be in in the morning. I can't do it." Harry mused as Mr. Johnson droned on about a case he was working on. Harry's mind was racing as he thought, "What about the three in my in-box, I haven't even touched. Doesn't he care about me or am I his slave? Oh, what a cruel taskmaster you are, Mr. Johnson!"

Again, Harry relaxed on his pillow and thought back over the three years since he had moved out of the research room and the multiple times he saw them take advantage of his skill and never offer to give him important cases to plead before the judge and a jury. It raised his anger and his blood pressure there in the hospital. Harry considered that as another reason to get out of the attorney career.

Gemme arrived to take Harry home and soon after, the head nurse came with the paperwork to release him from the hospital. As he was reading and signing the papers, she perused the room for personal belongings.

Gemme got into the hospital closet in his room and retrieved the clothes that he was wearing when he came in. Harry gingerly pulled up his pants and Gemme bent over and slipped his brown socks and penny loafers on his feet.

Just as he finished dressing, the nurse barged in pushing a shiny stainless-steel wheelchair. First, she had him sit on the bed while she checked to see if Harry had the "x's" in the mandatory boxes on the paperwork. "Harry, this looks good," she said as she slid them into her clipboard. "Climb in! Let's get you home," she happily ordered.

Meekly, he carefully backed up to the wheelchair. The nurse had safely locked the wheels. He sat down carefully, thinking it would feel good to be outside. Later at the front entrance of the hospital, they waited as Gemme brought the car around.

The nurse mused aloud, "We're outside the hospital, now you can walk. The wheelchair was hospital policy, you know."

At home, Gemme quizzed, "Are you hungry? And do you want to eat now?"

"Yes. It will be good to taste food that has been seasoned, not that old bland stuff from the hospital."

With the meal done and dishes washed, Gemme re-entered the living room and sat next to him on the sofa. To start a conversation, she asked, "Harry, have you done some thinking about your future while you were laying there in the hospital?".

"Honey, I sure did! If you're ready, I'll ty to explain why I'm close to saying I want to quit the law firm and being an attorney even through I've spent most of my professional years at it." He looked over just in time to see her nod her head yes. "Well, counting my apprenticeship of two years as a clerk. I have spent too many years and I don't seem to be any closer to moving up the ladder to senior partner. I've mistreated my body by working lots of twelve-hour shifts and some sixteen-hour days at the office. While pulling those long days, I ate lots of snacks and unhealthy food. I also left you home alone many days for which I am now very sorry." Then he stopped to catch his breath and try to remember the other reasons he didn't like being a lawyer. Gemme was eager to hear more.

Harry took a deep breath and slowly exhaled then started again. "Here's some other reasons why I have decided not to pursue senior partner. My goal of a big house only brings with it lots of upkeep. The money we've invested brings with it worry about the fluctuation in the stock market. I now realize having the latest electronic gadget and the most recent model car aren't that important. As a lawyer, we are continually being evaluated by everybody and that is irritating. People have the opinion all lawyers are rich and expect them to be very generous to every charity. One last thing is I am not sure I want to always represent people who do wrong and expect me to bail them out of the consequences that they rightfully deserve. Surely, there are upstanding people we could sincerely enjoy associating with." He was tired and wearily leaned his head back.

Gemme took his leaning back as a sign he had given all the information he wanted to give their first night home.

That night they both slept well. Gemme had to go into work the next morning, but she promised to bring home a meal from Ritzy's. She knew they could meet his new dietary requirements. "Harry," she questioned, "can we have another extended session after dinner about our future?"

"Certainly, Honey," he assured her.

The day went fast for Gemme, but Harry got tired about one o'clock and took a nap which lasted until an hour before Gemme came home with a grilled chicken dinner. The enticing aroma followed Gemme more strongly than her favorite perfume.

For Harry there was no talking business, even that of their future while the chicken's aroma found its way through the house. Gemme had not seen him eat so heartily in a long time. Between the two of them, there were only bones and empty containers when they finished. Since there would be no dishwashing, Harry volunteered to help clean the dishes. Hand in hand they exited the kitchen. Again, Harry eased into the overstuffed chair while Gemme took her customary place on the sofa.

In a voice of a dreamer, Harry softy let out, "I've always liked being a winner. I fondly remember as my baseball team in high school got on our bus to ride to Indianapolis. What a thrill! Even more joyful was when we stepped off the bus in the front of the team's booster club carrying the first-place trophy for the entire state of Indiana."

Questioningly she asked to see where Harry was in his thinking, "Are we thinking of moving to … New York City or some isolated place?"

It was a straightforward question, but dreamily he replied, "I hadn't thought about moving. Maybe we could downsize our family budget by moving somewhere locally.

Quickly she answered, "Good! I love my hometown of Evansville. Since you said we aren't planning on moving away, I can start thinking of what we can do here in Evansville." Gemme's position softened as she began to relax and lean back on the sofa.

Harry picked up the conversation by saying, "Like I said yesterday, I feel like I am not truly helping by assisting the guilty people get out of paying the consequences of their voluntary actions." That thought hung in the air for several minutes. Gemme was deep in thought as well. Harry again confessed, "I want to be around you and our friends that I **want** to associate with. I want to spend more family time with you."

"Can we **truly** help people?" Gemme asked, "You were as a lawyer helping people, but it seemed like the wrong kind of help," Gemme remarked. Then she continued, "In college I read of a motivational speaker who said that all of us should, 'Find a need and fill it.' Hopefully, you and I can find one."

Harry heard her but was still thinking about what would be good for him. "Gemme, I think I would want a job where I make my own decisions. I know I would be rewarded for the correct decisions as well as live with the painful results if I made the wrong ones. At the law firm, I have never made a decision of any consequence. And, … Honey, I want a job with some stress but not constant stress like I've had at the office."

Now it was Gemme's turn to think about what she really wanted in a job. "I have always had a sympathetic spot for animals and people when they were in need. Even in school, I helped friends out when they had a problem." Then Gemme put forth a genuine idea, "Harry, what do you think about helping needy people by starting a homeless shelter?"

Harry immediately looked up at Gemme. He smiled at her, "That is a wonderful idea. I have a lovely wife and a smart one, too."

She immediately came up with a negative but practical problem. "But how are we going to support ourselves?"

After Harry finished slowly scratching his head, he gave his answer. "We have enough to live on for possibly a year, … if we stretch it. If you don't mind, you could keep your job until we get the support of the town behind us."

They both agreed on the idea of a homeless shelter. They then headed to the kitchen for a snack to celebrate their decision. Gemme came up with a suggestion, "Harry, why don't we visit my folks and run our decision past them before you submit your official resignation to the Fleming & Johnson Law Firm, okay?"

He agreed. What a profitable evening!

It was several days later, one afternoon when Harry was enjoying a sip of tea and thinking about how things used to be at the office. He thought of the recent case he handled. It was of a landlord who was skimming his tenants and coming back to them claiming they were $10 or $20 short even though they had fully paid. Harry won the case in the landlord's favor. But he now recalled how badly he felt about the depressed looks of the tenants as they walked out of the courtroom. Harry had another sip of tepid tea with a squirt of lemon in it then settled back again into this lounge chair. How good it felt now to relax and not look at a half dozen cases to work with immediate time constraints.

Slowly, he faded back into a half sleep. It is a joy to work with Gladys and the rest of the crew, but at the same time depressing to work for the law firm. Harry remembered how Mr. Johnson, without qualms, had been giving him more and more work. It was as though he enjoyed making Harry, the newbie, be repeatedly loaded with extra work. "One day Mr.

Johnson left me with huge amount of work and went to the Country Club. Oh, how angry I was!" Harry recalled.

His body twitched and woke him up. He got up and walked in the yard to enjoy the garden of flowers.

5

New Career

> "Four things for success: Work,
> Pray, Think, and Believe."
>
> ~ **Norman V. Peale**

It was Thursday evening dinner at Gemme's folks. Gemme's mother had prepared pot roast, vegetables, and of course mashed potatoes. And there was red-eye gravy from the bottom of the pot where the roast had cooked. Harry enjoyed a little of everything but not as big of portions as before. Oh! Harry was able to eat a very small slice of his mother-in-law's fresh apple pie.

After Gemme and her mom had cleared the dishes and had removed the serving dishes they refilled everyone's coffee cup.

Gemme's father opened the conversation by asking, "What's this I hear about you changing occupations?"

Harry was eager to give his side of the story. They knew part of his answer as Harry was fairly sure Gemme had been talking with her mom. "Well, the stressful job I had as a lawyer contributed to my heart attack. So, I've been thinking about changing. I may have wasted the first half of my life as a lawyer. I'm contemplating trying some other job that I would enjoy and one with much less stress plus real enjoyment. Since the law firm has granted me an extra thirty days' leave with pay, I have time to think about it."

Gemme jumped into the conversation to relieve Harry. "Dad, we both like helping animals and people. Oh, remember all the stray cats I brought home?" Her dad nodded in total agreement. "We are seriously thinking about helping the homeless. We aren't sure how yet, but for sure there would be a lot less stress on Harry and bring both of us satisfaction that we are making our world better than we found it."

Her dad cleared his throat with serious authority and came forth with an important question. "Harry, if you go through with this, how are you going to support my daughter?"

Slowly Harry replied, "Sir, I've thought about that problem and don't have a clear answer for you. I just know other folks are making it while helping the poor and I have faith I will provide the necessities your daughter needs once we have the support programs in place with the good citizens of Evansville."

While looking at Harry, Gemme stood up and asked, "Babe, think we better head home? And … Mom, that was an excellent meal." The two of them left feeling they had their blessing except for the finances.

It was about a week later at Schnuck's Grocery Store when Gemme ran into Julie, an old high school friend. They had time to converse in the aisle and Julie was very interested to hear of Gemme's idea of a homeless shelter. "You know as police dispatcher, lately I have gotten more than the usual number of calls for vagrancy," Julie told her.

Gemme could hardly wait to tell Harry about her conversation with Julie and the growing need for a homeless shelter. At dinner that night, she filled Harry in with what Julie had said.

He promptly replied, "That is almost like a sign from God that we are to follow through with our plans."

Gemme agreed. That news was a clincher for her, too.

The extra thirty days of leave was coming to an end, so Harry had to decide to go back to Fleming & Johnson Law Firm as an employee or to resign.

"Honey, could you come into the dining room? We have discussed our future. Didn't we decide that I would resign?"

"Babe, I am convinced that would be the best decision for the rest of our lives. Are you needing help writing the resignation letter?" Gemme inquired.

"Well … not really. I just wanted us to solidly agree on the change in our lives. Once we break ties, there is no going back. And … the future may be filled with a boatload of trials and problems and maybe even times of little or no money." Harry said.

"Harry, I am ready for the change. The crises shouldn't be much harder for me than the long hours you spent at the office and leaving me all alone. I didn't complain, but it was real torture some evenings," she truthfully admitted.

"Thanks for confirming **our** decision. Now, I feel comfortable writing the resignation." As he bent over the yellow tablet, the pen fairly flew over the page. It was about an hour later when Harry pulled out his trusty laptop computer and it wasn't long before Gemme heard the printer in the other room wake up and begin printing.

Shortly thereafter, Harry came in holding two sheets of paper. "Gemme, would you read this over and edit it for us?" Harry recalled her excellent editing skills of his college papers and felt warm and glad he had married Gemme. She only added two commas.

When Monday morning came, Harry got up a little earlier than usual to read over his resignation once more and gave some thought to how to present it to Mr. Fleming. In a congratulatory way, Gemme had wished Harry good luck before she stepped out the front door to the adult learning center.

At his usual time to leave the house for work, Harry put his resignation in a manila folder and carefully placed it in his hardly used attaché case. Thinking to himself, Harry said, "Soon I will be starting a whole new era of my life. The change doesn't seem too heavy or scary right now. I am glad that Gemme and I reached this agreement together."

As this was Harry's first day back to work after his heart surgery, he parked in the lot and walked around to the front door, opened the big glass door and immediately said, "Good morning, Gladys." This walk in felt like a dream or Déjà vu. Immediately, the paid staff crowded around Gladys' desk and Harry. All kinds of questions flew; "How are you feeling? Did you enjoy your time off? We all sure missed you! There was a lot of extra work for all of us to do since you were gone."

Harry began to try to answer some of their questions. He was really pleasantly surprised at the enthusiastic welcome back to work by his co-workers.

To give Mr. Fleming time to settle in, Harry went to the faithful 30-cup office coffee pot that Gladys so conscientiously kept ready. After filling his favorite mug, he sat down and leaned back in his chair. Harry so badly wanted to tell Gladys his intentions, but he didn't want all the office staff to know before Mr. Fleming. That would not be proper. He did succeed in restraining himself.

When Harry's coffee was lukewarm, he decided it was time to bolster his courage and give his rehearsed speech. Hopefully, he wouldn't have to change it much. Harry tapped lightly on the doorpost. "Come in, Harry," Mr. Fleming invited. "It is good to have you back. How are you feeling? What's on our mind?"

Slowly Harry started into his speech. "Well … Mr. Fleming, I appreciate the years I've worked with you and Mr. Johnson. During the last month, I have been evaluating my life, I mean, our lives. Gemme and I have decided we need a life with less stress. So, today I want to give my two weeks' notice to resign." Then Harry handed Mr. Fleming his typed resignation.

Mr. Fleming was stunned and asked, "Harry, are you sure you've thought this through very carefully?" After adjusting to the sudden news, he continued, "Just the other day Mr. Johnson and I were discussing making you a senior partner."

Mr. Fleming desperately hoped Harry would change his mind. After carefully reading the letter for several minutes and not receiving a comment from Harry, Mr. Fleming realized that Harry had truly made up his mind. "I wasn't ready for this Harry, but Mr. Johnson and I will make up a generous severance package for you."

Harry spoke up and said, "Mr. Fleming, I appreciate that."

Mr. Fleming nervously drank a sip of coffee and then spoke, "Have you decided what you might do?"

Harry was more relaxed now sitting in a client's chair. He sat up straighter and explained how he and Gemme were thinking of starting a homeless shelter.

Mr. Fleming said, "If you need any help, feel free to call on us. I'm not sure how much financial help we would be able to give." Mr. Fleming shuffled some more papers and commented. "For the next two weeks we will take your cases, but you can help get cases ready for court. Have a good day. Harry, it has been good having you as a hard-working member of our firm."

Harry rose and walked out. He grabbed his coffee cup and refilled it and headed straight for Gladys. He told her the news that had been rolling around in his head all morning begging to get out.

"Oh, Harry I hate to see you go. I've seen how hard they have worked you and how diligently you've worked. I can't blame you," Gladys commiserated. "I wish you the best of luck."

Harry responded, "I'll be around for two weeks and maybe break in the new employee."

His news spilled out into the office as rapidly as navy beans out of a broken sack.

The two weeks flew by. Each night he and Gemme decided on potential ways of starting their homeless shelter.

6

First Shelter

> "Successful people are not gifted;
> they just work hard.
> They succeed on purpose."
>
> ~ **G. K. Nelson**

Now that Harry had time on his hands, he began thinking about housing for the homeless. His neighbors probably wouldn't allow homeless persons in their upscale neighborhood so he thought about purchasing a two-story house with several bedrooms and a bath upstairs and down. While he and Gemme lived on the ground floor, the homeless could live in the rest of the house. It had to be in a neighborhood that wouldn't pitch a fit with the city council over the clientele they would have plus stay within the zoning ordinances.

Before Gemme left for work, she gave Harry a heavy thought to chew on. "How are you going to entice a bank to loan you the money?" she asked and with a kiss she headed out the door and to her job at the adult learning center.

"I'll have another cup of coffee," Harry thought to himself, "Then I'll think on her question." A few sips later he thought about what assets they did have. Thinking aloud he considered, "We have the equity of our big house to use as a down payment and we could consider using the money in the severance package from the law firm. That may not be enough since we won't have a steady income except for Gemme's part-time job. For the bank, I will be a very poor risk. Another obstacle is I don't have a track record with this new adventure. The bank still may not okay me. What else might they ask for?"

As he drained the decanter of the 12-cup Mr. Coffee, an idea popped into his head, "Maybe Mr. Fleming might possibly consider cosigning the loan. That is worth a thought and may be our answer. I'm pretty sure Mr. Johnson wouldn't."

That evening he explained that day's reasoning to Gemme. When he finished, she was in favor of it and no frown on her beautiful face. After that, Harry kept his antennas up for any further suggestions from his dear wife.

The next morning as Gemme was about to leave for work she asked, "Harry, where are you going to look for the ideal home for us to start our new career?"

"I'll go to the older section of Evansville, that part is between the land north of the Ohio River and the Lloyd Expressway. I'll look in that area. There are some well-kept older homes there that would be ideal."

Later he showered, shaved and dressed to go on a private

expedition. In his imagination, he put on his pith helmet as he slipped behind the wheel. What a pleasure to be free to locate a house instead of heading to a pressure-cooker attorney's job. But, … he truly did miss the staff there who had so faithfully supported him.

Trusting God to lead him, he turned on Route 41 and headed south toward River Drive. From there all roads from Route 41 to Fulton Drive were roads that might have a house that would meet his needs.

Harry made several trips up to Lloyd Expressway and back south to the river. On one of the trips, he turned up Kentucky Street. He had just crossed St. Louis Street when he saw a two-story frame house with new vinyl siding. It was in a suitable area that allowed multi-family housing and he hoped wouldn't mind if a few homeless lived there.

Glory be! There was a bright red and blue Re-Max sign in the front yard signifying it could be bought. It was a nice house, so he ended his expedition for the day. Before he left the area he took a couple of quick pictures with his iPhone and made it back home before Gemme arrived. Harry couldn't wait to give Gemme the news of the great find on the first try to find a house that would meet their needs.

"Honey, how much does it cost?" she immediately quizzed when he gave her the news and showed her the photos.

"I don't know. I'll call now and then plan on making an appointment with Re-Max for an hour after you get home from work tomorrow. That will give us time to go by and get a look at the house before we meet with them. Does that sound okay?

Oh, by the way, tomorrow morning I'll stop by the law office and see if I can convince Mr. Fleming to cosign the loan."

She carefully looked over Harry's pictures again, slowly. She tried to digest all that was taking place at racetrack speed. Hesitantly, she mumbled, "Yeah, that is okay, I guess." She sincerely hoped they were heading in the right direction.

After the law office opened the next morning, Harry called and Gladys cheerfully answered. As soon as she found out it was Harry, her voice went up a few notes well mixed with much enthusiasm. Gladys was full of questions about how things were going with his new life. Finally, she gave Harry a chance to explain why he called.

"Gladys, I would like a fifteen-minute time slot this morning with Mr. Fleming if you can arrange it with him." Then he waited.

"Harry, I'll get right on that. Do you want me to tell him what it's about?"

"No, just tell him I'm not suing anyone and give him one of your great smiles, then I know he will be able to work me in."

"For you, Harry, I'd even twist his arm," she joked. "Oh, I have your phone number and I'll let you know as soon as I have something scheduled."

After they hung up, Harry had hardly gotten his second cup of decaf coffee poured when his phone rang with Gladys on the line.

"Harry, he said about ten o'clock would be fine. Come a little before your appointment and we can have our break time a little early and you can talk to all the gang."

"Okay," Harry replied. He was happy to have the appointment so promptly and looking forward to spending a few minutes with the staff.

"I'll be sure to have a freshly washed coffee cup for you." Gladys added. "See you then."

It was just 9:30 when Harry walked in. This time it was not to work but relax with friends. Oh! What a relief it was. Like a waitress, Gladys poured Harry a steaming hot cup of coffee. By then everyone was shaking his hand or patting him on the back and all of them bending his ear. He was as pleased to see them as they were to see him.

All too soon it seemed, Mr. Fleming walked out of his office as a signal he was ready for Harry and extended his hand and Harry shook it. "Come on in," he invited as he headed toward his desk, "What's this about? Are you dissatisfied with our severance package?"

"Oh, no," Harry started, "I am more than happy with it. I come asking a great favor of you. I found a perfect house to start our shelter program for the homeless. The equity in our house and the generous severance package will not be enough though. I will need to take out a loan. I'll need a reputable person to guarantee the repayment of the loan. I was hoping you would cosign the loan. It will simply be a formality as the mortgage will be very small and my payments manageable for me." Harry leaned back and paused to give Mr. Fleming time to consider the request. Harry could almost see the wheels spinning in Mr. Fleming's mind. He hoped he had phrased his request in an informative manner.

"I would be glad to cosign," he spoke with conviction. "I have seen that you are a determined person and a hard worker. I'm so glad I can help with such an important project for our community."

Harry popped up out of the chair like he had just sat on a thumbtack. "Thank you," he said as he reached to grab Mr. Fleming's hand. "Thank you, thank you," he repeated. Harry was so glad he had left under favorable conditions and not burned his bridge behind him. They agreed to meet at the bank when an appointment was scheduled and the final papers were ready to sign.

His business with Mr. Fleming completed, Harry bid everybody goodbye and even gave his old friend Gladys a firm hug. He thanked her again for arranging his meeting so promptly.

That afternoon he and Gemme slowly drove by the prospective house as they headed to the Re-Max office. They were both on cloud nine to have such a nice start and were feeling optimistic.

Their appointment was with a Mrs. Kelly Von Warner whom they had spoken with on the phone when they were inquiring about the asking price of the property. Mrs. Von Warner came out and shook their hands and ushered them to her office.

They spent some time going over the details of the property, the seller's price and necessary repairs that needed to be completed. It was within Harry and Gemme's estimated price range and they felt confident they could get the necessary financing.

Mrs. Kelly Von Warner said, "I'll see the owner. Next would be to check about your loan. I know the loan officer and can help there too. You can see her at the Old National Bank in the morning and maybe by Friday we can complete this sale."

It rarely happens, but in this case, they completed buying the house in one week. That was the first miracle in their new career.

7

Welcome

> "Success is when you look back on your life
> and the memories make you smile."
>
> **~ Selected**

With the home purchased, the first order of business was to apply for not-for-profit status from the Indiana State government. It allows an organization or group with a governing board of directors to operate legally. Harry had already invited and received confirmation of the seven persons who would serve as directors of the Homeless Shelter. This step was easy to complete.

Gemme and Harry worked some three evenings to fill out the required State of Indiana not-for-profit form they had downloaded. After finally completing the form, since Gemme was now working full-time, Harry made the trip of 170 miles to Indianapolis to personally submit the application.

Once Harry found the right building, he took a number

from the counter and waited to be called. After he was called, he and a government rep worked for two hours together on the necessary forms. Harry was then told to go to a waiting area until the computer spit out the completed document. About quitting time, the rep finally called him in again. This time they handed him the completed and stamped State of Indiana not-for-profit form. Harry merrily skipped out of the office and down the stairs to his car. As soon as he sat down in the car and took a breath, he called Gemme on his cell phone with the good news that the application had been approved.

She was glad, but added, "Harry, it's late. Get yourself a motel room for the night and drive back tomorrow so you can drive safely back to me. I love you, dear and I'm so glad this step has been completed."

Harry complied. The next morning, he started back from Indianapolis and got as far as the town of Spencer where he stopped for a late breakfast. This laid-back breakfast sure was different from when he worked at the law firm with hurried up meals, 44 oz sodas, dry sandwiches and salty snacks. "I like this!" Harry softly whispered to himself as he finished his meal and paid the cashier.

Harry was anxious to arrive home to be with Gemme. That evening he joyously invited her to dinner so Gemme freshened up with a favorite dress and a dressy jacket. "Where are we going to eat? she inquired.

"Well… I plan on taking us to BruBurger over on Main Street in the old Greyhound Bus Station."

"Oh, Honey that's a ritzy place," Gemme joyfully exclaimed.

"But this is a special occasion and calls for a lavish meal," Harry explained. So that night they celebrated another step on their success in the new season of their lives, no longer spending 12-hour days at the office.

Now it was time to begin work on their federal application for a 501c3 for the homeless shelter, a not-for-profit organization. It consisted of 103 pages which Harry and Gemme poured over page by page. Gemme spent three additional evenings checking blank spaces and sentences for completion or noticeable errors. The completed application was finally sent Registered Mail to Washington, DC.

Ten days later Harry received a registered letter. It gave notice that their application had been received and that a Jennifer Webb, a federal agent, was assigned to him for the 501c3. She scheduled to meet Harry there in the Evansville Court House in room 305 at 9:00 am on Friday.

Harry was nervous until he met her, but this rather tall slim brunette was kind and friendly, not brash and aggressive like he feared. She went through the application with him. She mentioned three items where Harry needed to furnish more detailed information. They scheduled another meeting for a month from then. Harry breathed a sigh of relief as he exited the courthouse and headed for his car. Gemme was relieved, as well when she heard the news when she arrived home that night.

It was the following Tuesday Harry got a call. Ms. Webb wanted the addresses and phone numbers of the board of directors. Harry thought she probably wanted to quiz them about the homeless shelter and their knowledge of the organization. Harry was glad to comply and was confident each would give a good report.

The next contact with Ms. Webb was a call that notified him and Gemme that all the work was done on the registration papers except putting the official stamps on and mailing it back to them. It had been many months since they had sent the application off.

The law office personnel heard about their exciting news and took up a gift collection and purchased a 12 place setting of china and flatware for the shelter-to-be.

Harry kissed his wife goodbye as he headed over to the shelter the next morning. As he backed into the street, he had a distinct impression that something significant was going to happen today.

Harry pulled into the shelter's gravel driveway and went into the house. The place seemed to be a mess. He began throwing trash into a plastic bag and after several hours, the place began to look better. He gathered up his bags and took them around back to the city trash barrels on wheels.

Then he thought, "I better check the front yard also for windblown potato chip bags and other trash." As he leaned over to pick up a piece of paper, he heard someone yell, "Hey, Harry How ya' doing?" Immediately, he straightened up and looked in the direction of the sound.

Harry told himself, "I don't know this guy." But, as the man got closer, he did recognize him. It was a high school friend he used to hang out with. "Well, if it isn't Jimbo Boyle. I never would have recognized you with that full beard. What brings you out this way?"

Harry extended his hand to Jimbo for a handshake. He hadn't gotten used to giving hugs yet to homeless people.

"Harry, I'm down on my luck. About six months ago I got fired from the factory. I searched and searched for another job and finally gave up. So here I am asking my best high school friend for help. Fred, our class president told me you were setting up a homeless shelter down here on the south side a couple blocks from the Ohio River."

"By the grace of God, I just happened to have an empty bedroom in the shelter, Jimbo, come on in." As he slipped his left arm over Jimbo's shoulder, they entered the shelter together.

8

Second Resident

> "Hard work doesn't guarantee success,
> but it improves its chances."
>
> ~ **B. J. Gupta**

Harry had spent the last few days in downtown Evansville looking for an additional person to fill an empty room at the shelter. This afternoon Harry was walking through a low rent section of town. He began asking several individuals how they were doing. Several perfunctorily answered, "Okay," to get this inquisitive man on his way. No one wanted to be truthful and tell their story of misfortune again and besides it was none of his business. Just as Harry was contemplating returning to his car, a young adult man with a full beard sidled up and inquired suspiciously why he was asking about everybody's welfare.

Harry slowly turned around and faced the young gentleman. "Well, my wife, Gemme and I run a homeless shelter on the south side of town. I'm searching for someone who needs a place to sleep. We presently have an empty room. Would you be needing a place to stay? It's free. But there are a few things we do ask. One, you keep your room clean and secondly, you search for a job to get back into society."

"Well, Mister, I have been wandering around for almost six years and the luster of being a vagabond has lost its appeal. If the offer still stands, I would be glad to go with you. By the way, my name is Roy," he said as he extended his chapped hand to seal the agreement.

"Roy, I'm Harry McKenzie. Let's go and get you started on your journey back to society." Harry was happy deep in his soul, because he was actually helping a fellow human being.

Harry and Roy arrived at the shelter just before the evening meal. "Roy, you can wash your hands in the bathroom down the hall. The towel on the rack is a community towel that gets washed often," Harry informed him.

When Roy returned, Jimbo was bringing the food in from the kitchen to the old-fashioned dining room. They all sat down, and Harry urged everyone to bow their heads as he offered the blessing.

Roy spied the steaming bowl of potatoes and baked chicken like his mom used to serve. He politely took some meat and a respectable serving of mixed vegetables. "What a delicious meal, Harry!" Roy announced. The other men at the table nodded their heads in agreement.

After the meal, Roy took his own dirty dishes to the kitchen. Jimbo asked, "Do you want to help clean up?"

Roy replied, "What do you want me to do?"

Then Jimbo answered, "Grab that dishtowel and dry these dishes as I wash them. Put them on the counter and I'll put them away."

From the other room Harry took note that Roy took the initiative in cleaning up after himself and helping Jimbo in the kitchen. That was a remarkable trait for a person who had been on the street for many years.

After he finished the dishes, Roy heard his name called. As he came into the dining room, Harry was looking at him. They walked up the stairs to the far room next to the bathroom. "Roy, this is your room. Each morning we expect you to make your own bed and pick up whatever is on the floor. Oh, Roy, and as I mentioned before our rule is that every day you hunt for a job or go to work. After you get a job, you donate some money to help pay the water, heat/air conditioning bill and groceries. Does that sound reasonable?" Harry asked, watching for his reaction.

"Sure, but I don't know if I'll ever get a job here in Evansville. I haven't worked in so long," he said as he threw his hands up in the air.

"Well … Roy, I plan on assisting you since it is scary getting started. First, if you don't mind, in the morning could you shave off your beard? Employers frown on that because it often hides facial expressions. Then while the other men go off to work, we'll go down to the Salvation Army Thrift Store and get you a suit." Harry giggled and put on a big smile. "No, not a suit just some presentable clothes and we'll wash the ones you have on," Harry informed him.

That night Roy slept soundly on a soft mattress which he

had not felt for a long time. The cardboard he was familiar with was a far cry from this real mattress.

The next morning just as Roy was getting ready with a pair of scissors to cut his beard and trim around his ears, Harry walked in the front door and yelled up the stairs. "Roy.... I stopped by the store and got you a new razor."

Roy looked like a completely different person at the breakfast table. He actually looked pretty handsome sitting there. Harry made that very comment after Roy had changed into his clean clothes. The Kix cereal felt good as it crunched between his teeth which he still had. He hadn't gotten into drugs. He had just wanted to drop out of society and leave the responsibility to everybody else. "Hopefully after Harry takes me to the Salvation Army for some new clothes, I'll be ready to look for a job," he thought to himself.

As they walked in the business district, Harry saw a sign in a restaurant window, "Help Wanted". Harry suggested, "Roy, I'll go in with you and let's apply for this job." Harry looked over at Roy. His face was blank. "I know, you would rather have a better job, but you have to hold a job awhile to establish a resume."

Begrudgingly, Roy grumbled, "Well...Okay."

The owner gave Roy a job application form. Harry noticed Roy read quickly and had fair penmanship. Harry volunteered, "Roy, you can use me for one of your references. Oh, I'll give you the address and phone number of the shelter when you get ready."

"Thanks," Roy replied with a faint smile realizing someone cared.

After he turned his application in, they headed home. In one of the lulls in conversation, Roy asked, "Harry, you have a dishwasher at the shelter. Why aren't you using it?"

"Well, it worked when we first bought the house, but it soon stopped," Harry explained.

It was an hour or so until dinner, Roy went down to the kitchen and wanted to check to see if the electricity was coming to the dishwasher, so he checked the switch box on the wall. Next, he opened the door to the dishwasher and peered inside. Then he pulled the entire washer out into the room being very careful not to kink the water line. He dabbled around underneath for a while, then shoved it back into its place and stood up and punched the start button. It started right up filling with water. Believe it or not, it went straight through the whole cycle.

"Roy, did I hear the dishwasher running?" Harry quizzed.

"Yup, there was an overload switch that needed to be manually reset," Roy calmly commented.

"Thanks, Roy," Harry declared, amazed at his talent.

From another room Jimbo yelled with enthusiasm, "We'll use it tonight."

Harry took note of Roy's mechanical ability to spot the problem when something is wrong. This potential might be helpful in getting him a job. It felt good to identify the positive in others instead of looking for human mistakes to win a case as an attorney.

That night the kitchen help was very pleased that the

dishwasher worked. It helped them get out of the kitchen sooner and up to their rooms to relax.

Roy hadn't donated any money yet to help pay the water bill, but he did save the repair bill on the dishwasher. This lifted Roy's spirits and he hadn't felt this good within since his high school graduation ceremony.

It was getting close to fall. Harry knew Ernesto of Greater Landscaping, a local company. He was a good Christian man and was often hiring. Many of his new employees didn't want to work hard so they didn't last long. "Let's try him tomorrow and see if he has any openings. What do you say, Roy?" Harry suggested.

"Well, I like that better than being dishwasher in a steamy restaurant. Okay!" his voice lifted with some enthusiasm. His life was changing.

Ernesto was tanned from a full summer of yard work. Although short, he had a commanding presence as Roy shook his hand. Ernesto thought that was good to have that kind of confidence, especially in a homeless person.

Ernesto immediately started questioning his possible new employee. "Are you afraid of hard work?" Then he leaned back against the company pickup truck waiting for an answer.

"Well, sir. I haven't worked hard in several years, but in a day or two I could hold up to a full, hard day's work." Roy thought that was an honest reply.

"The next question I always ask is can you and will you show up for work on time every morning, even Saturdays? I never work Sundays and I don't expect my employees to either."

Nervously Roy stammered again, "Well ... yes. To get me started I may have to enlist Harry's help. But I'm determined to try to be regular and a good worker." Roy kind of muttered loud enough for Ernesto to hear, "I haven't been regular at much since high school."

"Sounds like you have some determination. That's more than many I have hired." Then he looked Roy in the eyes and proclaimed, "You're hired. I'll see you Monday morning. Be here at eight. Oh, by the way, you'll need boots and not those tennis shoes you have on."

"Yes, Sir. Thank you, Sir. I'll be here promptly with boots on." Roy exclaimed with a broad smile that Harry had not seen before.

Harry shared the joy with Roy. Oh, how Harry enjoyed this feeling of helping others help themselves not just searching for mistakes and errors others had made as he did at Fleming & Johnson Law Firm.

When Monday came, Roy was at Ernesto's with hair combed and a clean-shaven face. Oh! Yes, with boots on directly from the Salvation Army.

By noon, Roy was tired and laid in the shade of the truck and took a quick nap during his lunch break. When a fellow worker awakened him, he felt much better. At the end of the day Ernesto asked Roy as he headed off to the shelter, "Can you stand another day?"

In a weak voice Roy replied, "It's hard work, but I can make it, ... I think."

That evening thoroughly exhausted Roy was so happy

he finished the day, even without complaining. Roy slept so soundly that he didn't hear the alarm go off the next morning and Harry came in about eight and shook him awake. Roy moaned, "What?"

"You're late for work," Harry informed him.

"Oh, no," he said as he tossed back his bedding. "I'll hurry and get ready. Would you take me straight to work? I promise I'll apologize to Ernesto," Roy blurted out. He felt like he had let Harry down.

"Sure," Harry confidently said. Inside Harry was proud of Roy. He was going from doing nothing to working hard and from doing what and when he wanted to a regular schedule.

Ernesto looked disappointed when Roy finally arrived but didn't say anything. Roy sincerely apologized saying, "I'm not used to working this hard."

"Okay, jump in the truck," as Ernesto smiled at Harry and gave him a thumbs up and slammed the truck door.

That afternoon one of the lawnmowers was cutting an uneven swathe. During a short break Roy asked, "Can I look at it?"

"Sure. Boys, help him turn that mower on its side," Ernesto requested.

Roy immediately saw the problem. "Ernesto, a chain link broke. Have we got a wire clothes hanger anywhere? I think that will hold up until you get it to the shop tonight."

"Sure, there is one in the truck probably behind the crew seat in the king cab," Ernesto informed him. So, with a pair of pliers, Roy fixed the mower temporarily, and they finished the day's work without the loss of any time.

Within a short time, Roy's muscles toughened up and he became a regular one of the crew.

At the end of October as the grass slowed its growth, Ernesto had to lay off some men. Since Roy was the last hire, he was the first dismissed. Ernesto commended him on being a good worker. "If you ever need a letter of recommendation, I'd be glad to write a good one for you," were Ernesto's parting words. "If you find yourself looking for work next spring, contact me."

Roy was so disappointed to have to tell Harry he got laid off, but that didn't affect his appetite for dinner.

The next morning the other men had vacated the shelter to go to their jobs. Harry and Roy sat on his bed and talked. Roy asked Harry, "Do you have any more ideas for jobs?"

"Roy, I've been watching you and assessing your skills. You have a knack for fixing things. Our school system is so big that they may have an opening. What do you say we go and see if there is job in the maintenance section of the Evansville School System? That is in the department that if something breaks down they send you over to get it running. How does that sound?"

"I'm not sure I can handle that big of a job." Roy halfway confessed.

"Let's try it," Harry enthusiastically encouraged. "Oh, let's write down Ernesto's address and my address for your references. You know that you really should have three references."

So, the two of them agreed and climbed into the vehicle and

headed to the administrative office of the Evansville School System. They walked in and were directed down the hall to the Human Resources office.

"Good morning," the lady in the office pleasantly announced.

"Ma'am, I'm here to apply for a job. I think I qualify for a job making broken things work," Roy boldly announced, with a big smile.

Harry quickly added, "As his sponsor, I agree. Even without formal training I recommend him."

Roy gave a noticeable sigh of relief.

The lady questioned, "Roy? Is that your name?"

"Yes, Ma'am," he politely replied.

"Just this week one of our maintenance men had hip surgery and will be out for twelve weeks. Please fill out the application form and I'll see what we can do to help you help us."

Roy sat down and filled it out. He had two references. After finishing, he sat there a little longer. Roy wondered if he should put his dad's name, J. D. Johnson as his third reference and his old home address. Oh, well! He finally decided, even though they hadn't spoken in over five years, he added it. He handed in his application.

The next day the school called and set up an appointment. Roy went in. The boss of the maintenance department smiled as he came through the door. "Roy, you're hired. What size shirt and waist do you have? We'll get you in a uniform with Evansville insignia on it as soon as possible," the boss said. "Now, let's go to a school that has a broken water fountain. We'll take the truck over. You can use my tool kit and I'll watch you fix it," the boss challenged.

"Yes, Sir," Roy replied. "I'm ready to go."

Every job the boss gave him for the next week he completed without any help or any problems. At the end of the month, the boss hired Roy full time with pension and health benefits. So, Roy soon moved out of the room at the shelter into his own apartment. Harry and Gemme were so proud that they took themselves to Shylers Barbeque and had a great dinner celebrating the joys of their new life.

9

Temporary Resident

> "The only place success comes before
> work is in the dictionary."
>
> ~ **Vince Lombardi**

Harry often visited the area where many of the homeless hung out. He always parked the van at the edge of the area and from there walked the two blocks on one side of the street and back on the other. He had learned that driving through the area was useless. Personal contact was most effective.

On this trip he noticed that the same tall and slender middle-fiftyish man was there that he had seen the last two walk-throughs. This time Harry had the urge to meet him personally. As he approached, Harry greeted him, "Hi, I am Harry. What's your name?"

The man carefully sized Harry up then snappishly answered through his full-face beard, "Why do you want to know?"

Taken off guard, Harry stepped back a pace and replied,

"Well … it's easier to talk using a man's name than just saying hey you." He continuing on, "I have a homeless shelter across town and was wondering if I could be of any help to you." Harry explained. "I'd like to talk to you about it."

"My name is Fred Prather," the bearded man said, in a friendlier manner, then held out his hand to Harry. "Glad to meet you. It is such a pleasure to meet someone who actually wants to help and not just be a do-gooder and leave." He continued, "I've tried to get a job, but no one needs my kind of help. I've been living on the street now for some time."

"The program at the shelter will help you get a job, if you are serious about getting back into society," he informed Fred.

"How do I join?" Fred inquired with some relish, anxious to get more information. Maybe his prayers were finally being answered.

"If you are ready, we could go now. I have the van at the end of the block."

Fred picked up his well-worn backpack which he had dropped next to his feet, turned and looked back at several men who had gathered a few feet away, turned around and said to Harry, "I'm ready."

After a twenty-minute drive across town, they came to the house-turned-shelter. By his expression, Fred seemed pleased with his first impression and remarked on the spaciousness and cleanliness of the house.

Harry presented the rules for living in the house, times of meals and about the requirements of keeping his sleeping area clean. Fred didn't sleep too soundly his first night for fear it wouldn't last.

The next day Harry and Fred headed out to try to find Fred a job. Over the course of the day, they put in six applications and had one interview. Then it was back home to a wonderful meal prepared by Jimbo and for the first time in a long time a quiet room Fred could call his own. The soft, clean bed called for Fred after he helped clean up the dinner dishes.

That evening shortly after supper, a job interviewer called for Fred and said the dishwasher job he wanted was open and he needed to be there by six am the next morning. Fred reluctantly agreed. He knew he had to be working in order to stay at the shelter and he wanted to stay. Fred showered that evening and set the alarm for five to be ready for the job.

When Harry called upstairs the next morning, Fred came down immediately, dressed casually but neatly. The day went well. Fred came home dragging that evening because he hadn't worked that hard in years.

The next morning Fred had just begun to get ready for work about the time he was supposed to be at work. When he did arrive, the owner frowned and was very disappointed with his late arrival. Fred put in another hard day, watching the clock as the hours dragged by. This was just not what he wanted to be doing.

The third morning when Harry called up the stairs, because Fred was running late again. Fred shouted down, "I'm not going."

Immediately Harry ordered, "Ok, get your backpack. I'm

taking you back to the place where I picked you up. You've broken the rules of the house. You agreed to work each day when a job was available to you. In order to live here, you must follow our rules.

Fred, with his backpack at his feet, rode in silence but didn't concede or apologize to Harry when he arrived back to his old home ground. He quietly let himself out of the van without even saying goodbye.

Harry headed back to the shelter disappointed but knowing full well it was Fred's responsibility and decision. He had tried his best to help him, but Fred had to be willing to do his part.

It was about a year later when Harry began seeing Fred again there in Evansville. That evening he talked to Gemme about taking Fred in again, if he really wanted to try again. They both agreed to give him another chance if Fred would once again agree to the rules. This had to be his last opportunity.

This time Fred knew what was expected of him and readily agreed. He knew he couldn't survive on the street much longer.

While job hunting this round, Fred found a job as a security guard with regular nine-to-five hours. He thought he could keep this job, and sure enough, he did keep it for several weeks. He made sure he was always on time, always in a clean uniform, and kept the rules both on the job and at the shelter.

One evening after dinner Fred sat down at the old upright piano that was left by the previous owner when Harry purchased the house and began to play. Oh! you heard the most beautiful swing music that ever tickled your ear drums! Fred was a very talented pianist and though he hadn't played in years, he could still master the keys.

Harry was amazed and convinced Fred would fit into the little neighborhood bar and lounge he knew near St. Joseph Street and Lloyd Expressway. He would see if the owner could use Fred to fill his place with beautiful soothing music for his customers. He was hopeful.

As soon as Fred got off work the next day, he and Harry made a stop at the lounge and introduced themselves. Pete, the owner and bartender was willing to listen to Fred play. Fred adjusted the bench and sat down. He played three different types of music: ragtime, jazz and a classical number. Pete was pleased with the music and impressed by Fred's neatly trimmed beard and security uniform. "Can you come tomorrow night at eight and play until twelve or one? Your pay will be seven-fifty dollars an hour and all the tip money the customers put in the fishbowl on the piano. If you are interested, slacks and sport shirt would be proper attire."

"Sir, I need to give my present job a notice, but I could come for a couple of hours in the evenings to get in practice and still get enough sleep for my other job."

They parted in agreement that Fred would return at 8 pm. He was a big success. Right after he quit the security job, it wasn't long before Fred moved out to his own apartment within walking distance of the lounge. Harry and Gemme had graduated another homeless shelter resident.

Several months later Harry thought he should check on Fred and take Gemme for a light supper at the same time. "Gemme, let's go to the lounge and check on our pianist. We haven't seen or heard from him in quite a while and I'm curious."

That night they dressed up to go out and as they entered the lounge, Harry nudged Gemme and asked if she could see who was sitting at the piano. "I hope Fred didn't get fired or quit," he said quietly. The music was being played very professionally but the piano was out of sight.

After they had enjoyed their meal on the other side of the dining room, they walked hand in hand over to the piano. When they were only eight or so feet away they still didn't recognize Fred as the piano player.

The pianist confidently stood to his full height when he saw them approach. "Harry and Gemme, it is so good to see you," Fred said as he threw his arms wide and gave Harry a polar bear hug and a gentler hug to Gemme. "It's so good to see you," he repeated. "I love my job here and the business has increased for Pete. I couldn't have done this without your help. You have completely changed my life."

"Fred, we didn't recognize you. You look great! We are pleased you are happy here and it shows! We simply gave you some resources to help out. Gemme and I are **so** proud of you."

10

Second Shelter

> "Don't look for shortcuts to success.
> Work harder than anyone else and never give up"
>
> **~ GYMquotes.Com**

For the third year, Gemme and Harry had been keeping the shelter at full occupancy. One night while Harry lingered at the dining room table after the meal, Gemme quizzed, "Babe, what's on your mind?"

"Well, … I have been thinking that it might be a good time to open a second shelter. We discussed this possibility some time ago."

Gemme knew he was right, but with the extra residents and extra expenditures she would have to reduce her hours at her job at the adult learning center workshop to have time to do the two shelters' books. "That will be a huge undertaking!" she continued, "I will have to go part-time, and we would have to live on much less income in addition to what we receive to support the shelter."

Their discussion continued into the evening, the talking ended with both fully convinced that the additional shelter was inevitable and was in keeping with their long-range goals. There would have to be a chronological plan laid out. Their accomplishments in their new life felt more satisfying than being promoted to Senior Partner in Fleming & Johnson Law Firm.

The next morning Gemme went to work and Harry saw that everyone at the shelter went to work also. It was important to keep the newer residents motivated so they didn't fall back into their old routines.

After the shelter cleared, and in the silence at the large dining room table, Harry took out his yellow tablet and started brainstorming about what needed to be done and listing the priorities:

1. Locate a suitable second house, nearby if possible.

2. See if it meets the zoning code for a not-for-profit organization.

3. Close on the house.

4. Have a community-wide fund raiser.

5. Renovate the house as necessary to meet shelter needs.

6. Have a grand opening and give a personal invitation to all donors and friends.

After completing his projected plan, he had a strong urge to swing by Gemme's place of work and show her his outline.

It was very important to Harry that she be on board with this order of priorities.

At the door she frighteningly quizzed, "Harry, what's wrong? You never come to my job."

"Nothing Honey, I just wanted you to see what I have outlined and if you like the sequence."

"Just a minute and we can go into the conference room, after I inform the staff," she said. As she reentered the room she asked, "Okay, what have you got?"

"These are six steps that might take us six to eight months to complete. We would then be in a new exciting stage of our career," he told her with a big smile.

Gemme bent over and quietly studied his plan carefully. "Well ... I think you are right on, except on step three. Will there be a large down-payment required to lower the mortgage payments or will we be depending on the fundraiser to provide enough funds? Would the bank okay a loan without a sizeable down payment?" Gemme was asking good questions.

Harry's smile was still pasted on his face because she hadn't disagreed but sharpened his projections.

Beginning that night and for two more months they scanned the realtor's pages in the *Evansville Courier*, looking for an appropriate house with enough bedrooms for their needs. Then one morning as Harry left the shelter, he noticed a house near the end of the block with a for sale sign in the yard. Harry's imagination spun almost out of control. "That house is larger and has two more bedrooms than we have. I couldn't have dreamed of a better house. It is well cared for plus near to the first shelter!" Then his enthusiasm slowed as he seriously contemplated, "I wonder what they are asking for it."

Well, he soon answered that question. Harry got on the Zillow website and found that the owner had purchased it for $198,000 ten years prior. After considering that the owners had lived there that period of time, he estimated the sale price to be in the $300,000's. The sale price was not listed.

That night Harry could hardly wait for Gemme to come home so he could share his news with her. She was as happy as Harry. Since she agreed, Harry called the realtor and set up an appointment to inspect the house. The neighbor that was selling was so happy to hear from the realtor that he had a nibble so quickly.

As soon as Gemme got home the following night, they met the realtor and drove over to look at the house. They loved it. The part they liked the best was the master bedroom and bath were on the first floor along with a second smaller bedroom. The other four bedrooms were upstairs and shared a bath and a half. Harry and Gemme would have to share their bathroom with Jimbo, their resident/caretaker, who would have the other downstairs bedroom, which wouldn't be a problem. The next day Gemme arranged to take two hours off of work so she and Harry could meet with the realtor again to see about actually purchasing the house.

"The owner is asking $300,000 for the property, sir. You will need ten percent down," the realtor announced with a smile.

Harry's heart sank. In his mind he was thinking, "How can I get my hands on $30,000? Oh, maybe I could make that smaller and ask if they would lower the price." Harry looked up at the agent. Without getting Gemme's permission, he spoke up, "I would like to offer him $225,000," Harry said with confidence in his voice.

The agent had Harry sign a purchase offer and agreed to tell the owner that evening.

As they drove home, Harry told Gemme that he had researched the previous sale of the house and the neighbor had paid under $200,000 for it. He also told her that the neighborhood was made up of similar style and aged homes, and that a $300,000 price tag was too much. They both felt this was a good low-ball bid.

The neighbor decided not to accept the bid, so Harry upped his bid to $250,000.

When the realtor called the next day and gave Harry notice that the neighbor had accepted his purchase offer by lowering his selling price by $50,000. Harry immediately accepted and arranged for him and Gemme to meet to sign the contract that Friday afternoon. He would have to contact Mr. Fleming again.

Harry now had another problem. He would have to renovate it to meet the city and state health codes. Hopefully, Jimbo, his high school buddy and resident supervisor would be able to do most of the changes except for electric and plumbing, which needed to be completed by a licensed contractor.

Again Mr. Fleming cosigned, and Harry was able to secure the loan for the second shelter, but the expenses of the first shelter were taking most of the present income. Therefore, Harry thought that this would be an appropriate time to host the fundraiser dinner they had on their prospective list. Besides the dinner meal, the advertisement might generate some continuous income to keep up with the daily expenses on the second shelter. Gemme and Harry set aside the entire day the following Wednesday, one of Gemme's days off from her part-time job at the adult day care to plan the fundraiser event.

That morning Harry had their 12-cup Mr. Coffee going earlier. They laid out their oversized 12-month calendar that resembled a tablecloth on the large dining room table. They planned to schedule when to start or complete each section of the fundraiser. Since Gemme's handwriting was neater, he had a brand-new yellow tablet and a Bic pen waiting for her.

The first item on the agenda was advertising. Gemme's pen began as she wrote down that the Evansville Courier was first. At her part-time job, she heard a radio in the background all the time. "I'll list the radio stations like: WIKY 104.1, WGBF 1280 FM and WNIN 88.3," she decided. "Can you think what television station would give us the most economical advertisement?" she asked Harry. "Maybe even a local public service spot?"

"My favorites are WFIE channel 15, then WEVV channel 44 and finally WEHT channel 7, not necessarily in that order."

Harry got up from the table, "I'm going for more coffee. You want a cup?"

"Oh, about half a cup will do me for now," Gemme replied.

As he started back, Harry thoughtfully announced that he also wanted the Evansville Chamber of Commerce listed. They had been so helpful on the first shelter. It was always sound advice they gave, not money.

Gemme suggested churches. "They are giving-type people who care about their community. We ought to include them."

"Well ...," Harry began, "The First Baptist Church, the well-attended Christian Fellowship Church, Oak Hill Christian Center, St. John United Methodist Church, the First Presbyterian Church and the St. Gregory Catholic Church on Pollack Avenue." Harry didn't realize it at that time that the St. Gregory Catholic Church would be making such a big impact on his fundraiser.

"Oh ...," Harry exclaimed, "when we approach businesses for a donation, we want to remind them it might give their company a corporate tax break."

Gemme popped up with the first two, "The electric company, Vectren and the Old National Bank in Evansville, and Banterra Bank."

"Yes, and Berry Enterprises, Fleming & Johnson Law Firm and possibly Evansville Teachers Federal Credit Union."

Gemme finished writing and the room returned to silence again. They were both quietly concentrating on thinking about other contributors.

It was several minutes before Gemme had another idea. "We should also think about inviting our friends. We could invite our high school friends, college friends and fellow workers we have had."

Harry was dry of any other sources for contributors. He

suggested they start on the menu and preparation, including appetizers, beverages, main meal and desserts.

Gemme started out first, "What are we going to have as the main course?"

"Well, I was thinking roast beef or sliced ham for an entrée, either baked potato or mashed potatoes and green beans Almondine or candied carrots. How does that sound?"

"Sounds like you've been thinking on an empty stomach," she smiled.

"Oh, Honey, the cooks could help decide which meat or potato, what menu would be within a budget and what cooking equipment is available at the venue."

Again, both thought in the silence except for the noise of the icemaker in the refrigerator dumping a load of ice and the strong aroma of the last few cups of coffee in the pot.

"Harry, my dad was a cook in the Navy, and he has a friend who was a cook in the Army. We could ask them to donate their time and talent and give us some advice. They would be familiar with cooking for large groups."

Harry jumped on that, "What a wonderful idea! We do make a wonderful team, don't we? Could we ask the youth group of the Christian Fellowship Church where we used to attend to be our servers? They could all wear a white shirt or blouse with dark slacks. It might look classy."

"Let's try that, Dear." Slowly … Gemme added, "… but what about the venue?"

"Oh, I hadn't forgotten. We just haven't gotten to it. My thoughts are to use Robert's Stadium though that might be very expensive to rent. We might have less profit even though it might draw more professional people," Harry conjectured.

From that day on, the pair were really busy as if they had an eight-hour day job. Gemme was collecting names and addresses, Harry kept the van hot seeing people and businesses. The first stop was the Christian Fellowship Church to see about using their fellowship hall. But, as it turned out, they were not booking non-religious groups at this time.

On the way back across town, Harry noticed the large cross on St. Gregory's Catholic Church. So, he turned right onto their street, parked and walked up to the door that read, "Pastor's Study" thinking he may as well start there. Looking up from her desk, the church secretary was very cordial and asked, "How may I help you?"

"I'm Harry McKenzie. My wife and I run the Homeless Shelter on the south side of Lloyd Expressway. We are wanting to have a fundraiser and would like to see about the use your fellowship hall and facilities."

"That sounds possible," she commented. "Could you fill out this form so if something gets broken, we know who to contact," she added. Then her face lit up with a broad smile as she rose and headed toward the door labeled "Pastor's Study."

About the time Harry completed the form, Father O'Malley stuck his head out his office door and asked him to come in. "Tell me about your organization and what you are aiming to accomplish," the priest asked after showing Harry to a comfortable chair in front of his desk.

After Harry's brief explanation of his homeless shelter,

Father O'Malley spoke, "Your fundraiser assists our church to reach out and that's what we are here for. I've heard of the work you've been doing with the homeless and I commend you. You are making a difference and I know it's often a challenge. Let's go down to the fellowship hall and check in the kitchen where the schedule is. You will be able to see what equipment we have and if your cooks need to make any other arrangements.

The calendar on the wall was like the one they used at the shelter. It had oversized squares for each day allowing for as many written details as needed. It looked well used here at St. Gregory's. "When would you like to use it?" Father O'Malley asked.

"Well, people are most generous between Thanksgiving and Christmas," Harry replied, "Let's look in that time frame and see what's available. A Friday or Saturday would be ideal, but even during the week might do."

"Jumping Jehoshaphat," the Padre expressed, smiling at his own expression. "Every possible time is filled." With raised eyebrows he turned around and looked questioningly at Harry.

"My next choice would be around Valentine's Day when all are thinking of love. That might work," Harry said craning his neck to look up at the calendar.

"Holy Smoke, Valentine's evening is open. God must be guiding you while you're helping us to reach out with God's wondrous love. I'll pencil you in. The final approval will of course come from the Board." He smiled again and gave a little chuckle. "They usually okay what I suggest since I'm head servant of the Lord around here," he said as that impish smile reappeared on his face.

"Thank you, Father for your help. We'll pray for you and your church and be in touch as we get closer to the date." Harry headed to the front door of the fellowship hall instead of going back through the church again noting the dimensions of the large space where their fundraiser would be held.

Back at the shelter Gemme continued to check the websites for contacts and phone numbers that would help them put their invitation list together. She was startled when Harry came barging through the door and in a loud voice shouted, "Let's go celebrate. Join me at Starbucks for coffee," and in a softer voice said, "You can have a Mocha light."

"Why are you so exuberant? You almost swept me off my chair!"

"I just got the fellowship hall at St. Gregory Catholic Church and guess when?" Without waiting for an answer interjected, "Valentine's night!"

"Oh, that is wonderful," Gemme said, "I have something to celebrate too. My dad and his friend confirmed they would take care of the menu and the cooking. We are making progress on this and the Lord seems to be blessing our efforts."

Agreed," Harry said, giving Gemme a hug. "Now, let's go get that special coffee!"

In the next few weeks, Gemme volunteered to keep working on the invitation list because she figured that only 30% of the invitations would yield a person who would come. She added to her list new friends whom their friends recommended. This helped tremendously.

Harry said he would see the Coke or Pepsi distributors about donations, then continue visiting area businesses and asking for help with advertisement.

Thanksgiving and Christmas came and went, and they were close to completion on all the preparations. The letters of invitation got mailed on time.

Gemme and Harry sat down one evening and gave some serious thought to the expected net they hoped to realize from the fund raiser. "If we ask $200 a plate and 100 guests come that would yield $20,000. My dad estimates around $500 to feed a group of 100 which amounted to nearly $5.00 a plate. Considering beverages donated that would net over $19,000 per 100 persons.

After months of meticulous planning and hours of phone calls and contacts the night of the big fundraising dinner finally came. Oh, the youth group had all the napkins, utensils and glasses immaculately set, and stood by ready to serve the tables of the attendees. The hall was beginning to fill and by 6 pm, every chair in the fellowship hall was filled.

Of course, Father O'Malley welcomed all those in attendance and explained the purpose of the dinner before he gave the blessing over the meal. Immediately after the blessing, the youth came out with a plate in each hand. They looked so professional with their coordinated outfits. It didn't take long to serve the entire hall. Everyone was pleased that the meal service was quick and the food was still warm.

The conversation slowed as everyone enjoyed their dinner of fresh warm yeast rolls, baked glazed ham, green beans Almondine, and choice of dessert of peach or apple pie ala mode. After all were finished eating and enjoying their coffee, Harry tapped on his water glass to get their attention.

"The shelter is so proud you came tonight." Harry greeted everyone and continued with a short history and a couple of success stories that related to individuals who had sought housing and now had full-time jobs and apartments of their own. In closing, he slowed down his delivery to get their attention, like he had learned to do as a lawyer before juries.

"Do we have any testimonials from our audience?" he asked, searching the faces of the guests. It wasn't long before a representative of Berry Enterprises stood up. "Our company is proud to hire people who have been through the program. The four we have hired have been hard workers and faithful to show up on time daily. This is a very worthwhile organization so be generous in your pledges," he said before sitting down.

Harry surveyed the audience, and quickly announced, "The pledge cards are near your plate."

A representative of a local plumbing business stood to be recognized. The stately-looking gentleman spoke in a firm voice. "My small company wants to pledge $1,000 in the next twelve months. I urge others of you to match or exceed that pledge to assist the shelter to give the homeless a 'helping hand up' back into society."

Harry spoke in an audible volume, "The cards can be placed in the boxes on either side of the door as you exit. There may be some who would like to think and pray about the amount of their pledge or contact your organization's financial officer. The mailing address is on the card and will go straight to the bank, Attn: Homeless Shelter, so 100% will go to the reduction of the loan on our second shelter. There may be a few of you who might want to help on a monthly basis, and we would graciously welcome your participation. Address your donation to the Homeless Shelter, on St. Louis and Kentucky Avenue. Thank you for coming and God bless each of you for wanting to help this important cause.

People immediately began talking in small groups as they began to fill out their cards and leave. Many were bragging about the good work of the Homeless Shelter. Almost everyone knew of someone who knew someone who had benefited.

Soon the room was empty except for the graduates of the Shelter who gladly volunteered to clean up. A church volunteer ran the dishwasher so nothing would get broken. Jimbo was bent over the deep double sinks scrubbing the big pots and pans which the cooks had used. They wanted to leave the church kitchen as clean as they had found it with everything back in its place.

One resident of the Homeless Shelter who was helping with the cleanup responsibly said, "I'm going to give an additional $20.00 every Friday to help with general expenses. Well, maybe more when I get my full-time job." Several voiced an 'attaboy' or 'good for you' in response.

The fundraiser was a success. When Harry and Gemme added up the pledge cards there was $25,530 plus the $20,000 from the meal tickets. Before the month was over, the bank had received additional pledges of $14,800. The final gross intake was a whopping $60,330 and donations continued to come in almost weekly.

Mr. Justin and Katie Jones, whom Gemme and Harry met some time ago at the country club gave a large donation. It was reassuring that they remembered the cause.

11

Another Resident

> "It always seems impossible, until it's done."
>
> ~ **Nelson Mandela**

One evening after chores were done at the homeless shelter, Jimbo decided to visit the area where the homeless usually gathered. The area all looked the same as when he lived there, and most of the people seemed the same. Jimbo waved to some and talked to others until he came to Joey, a tall, thin man in his 40's with prematurely gray hair and beard. He looked more dejected than Jimbo remembered. "Joey, where is your sister, Alice?" Jimbo inquired.

Slowly with his sad eyes he looked up at Jimbo, "Well … Alice died last year and now I'm all alone," Joey replied and then turned and looked down again.

"Are you making out alright? I mean are you using food stamps and do you have a place to sleep?" Jimbo quizzed.

"I'm all right, I guess, but I really do miss my sister. I have no one to care about me since she left. I have been so lonely, Jimbo, thanks for asking." Joey graciously and softly answered.

"I care about you. I recall when we were together down here. You, Alice and I used to share meals and talk about things. Since I left, I have found a homeless shelter that treats me well and with respect. I could ask Harry, the man who runs it, if they might help you. Would you like that?" Jimbo asked.

"Jimbo, I'm getting along well enough here except during these Indiana winters. They're awfully cold. Do you really think I could handle the change?" Joey inquired.

"Well, I'm going to be asking, but I'm not promising anything you know," Jimbo said giving himself room in case Harry and Gemme said no.

Jimbo turned to leave. "Take care," he told Joey.

Joey meekly and softly replied, "You too," as he watched Jimbo walk away leaving him alone and cold.

The next evening after dinner Harry walked into the kitchen while Jimbo was doing the dishes. Jimbo addressed Harry, "Hey, Harry, yesterday I ran into Joey, an old friend of mine from the streets. He recently lost his sister, Alice, and seemed so depressed. The next time we have a vacancy at our shelter could we see if we can take Joey in?"

Harry immediately replied. "Yes," because it meant he could provide help for one more life. Doing that gave Harry such a pleasant feeling inside, which he had never experienced in his career as a lawyer.

It was another two months before one of the residents was making enough money to pay the rent on their own apartment plus groceries and spending money and was moving out. There would be room for a new resident.

One afternoon, Harry remembered his conversation with Jimbo. "What was that fellow's name you said his sister had died and left him all alone?"

"His name was Joey. Do you want to interview him, and can I use the van to pick him up?" Jimbo enthusiastically quizzed.

"How about tomorrow after dinner. Gemme will be off work and maybe we both can make an immediate decision." He assured Jimbo he could use the van to go get him.

The next evening Jimbo arrived with Joey. Gemme saw he was unbathed and had soiled clothes. She had become accustomed to this. The part that truly bothered her was that Joey seldom looked up and conversed while looking down. The immediate question in her mind was, "Does he have a mental problem? We can't afford a liability like that, nor do we have the resources to help him." The interview continued a while longer, then Jimbo took Joey back to his regular spot downtown without a clear answer of whether he could come to live with them at the shelter or not.

It was a whole week before Harry was ready to give Joey an answer. He and Gemme decided Joey was only severely depressed and that he wouldn't be a liability. They believed he was a person they could help back into society.

Jimbo had painted the walls of the recently vacated bedroom and hung the new curtains Gemme had bought. Oh, yes, and Jimbo washed all the bed linens and the bedspread so the room was ready for their new occupant.

Harry said, "Jimbo, tomorrow morning you can go get Joey if he still wants to come live here and show him his new quarters."

As soon as the other residents left for work Jimbo went to pick up Joey and together they walked into the shelter. Harry greeted, "Come on in, Joey. Have a seat on the couch with your friend Jimbo. We hope you will feel at home here." Harry went over the rules: keep your room clean, help with the dishes or meal preparations. When you get a job, you are urged to contribute a small amount to help run the shelter until you can move into an apartment of your own. There is to be no alcohol, smoking or loud music, and you are encouraged and welcomed, though not required, to attend church services when you can."

Joey agreed to the rules and looked forward to meeting the other residents at the end of the day when they returned from their various jobs.

Jimbo volunteered to carry his plastic grocery bag of personal belongings up to his room and get Joey settled in. He showed him to the bathroom and shower and offered a clean set of clothes so he could launder what he was wearing.

The next morning Jimbo made sure Joey was up in time for breakfast. Joey enjoyed his food but didn't join in the conversations. Jimbo urged the other residents to give him some time to adjust.

Harry immediately put Joey on the list for a job, but he was a poor risk for an employer in his depressed state. Within a week, Jimbo had him helping with the yardwork to keep him busy.

One day Harry mentioned that the second homeless house could use a new coat of paint. First, parts of the weatherboard would need to be steel brushed to remove loose paint. Joey volunteered and did an extraordinary job. Believe it or not, when the painting was completed, one of Harry's neighborhood friends asked who painted his homeless shelter. After he told him it was two of his residents, the friend hired Jimbo and Joey to paint his house. Joey seemed to be recovering nicely from his depression and looking forward to a little more participation each day. Harry felt the increase in physical exercise was helping.

Shortly after the house painting, Joey attained a part-time job with the local veterinarian, Dr. Trent. The job was cleaning cages and was only from 8-12 each morning.

Joey loved the job and worked comfortably with all the animals. He didn't have to worry about unwelcome confrontations with people. One day when a new dog came in, the name on her cage read, "Suzie, Pomeranian". He visited her cage often each morning. Dr. Trent observed and offered to let Joey walk her once each day before going home, if all the cages had been cleaned. Dr. Trent noticed Joey was more fulfilled with Suzie and mentioned that to Harry. He also told Harry that Suzie was a stray and would soon have to be euthanized if she couldn't find a home. It would be helpful to him if Joey could adopt her.

This was a new wrinkle for Harry to decide on animals in the shelter. Gemme's conclusion was that as long as it contributed to Joey's well-being, it would be okay.

That evening Harry was listening to Joey talk about his day's experiences at the veterinarians and asked, "Joey, would you like to adopt Suzie? It sounds like the two of you get along well."

A smile lit up Joey's face as if this was a whole new idea

and Dr. Trent hadn't mentioned it to Joey. "Sure would!" He quickly replied with a bright energetic voice and excitedly looked directly at Harry.

"Now, you know there are responsibilities with this adoption," Harry told Joey. "You have to feed her each morning and evening, buy dog food, and walk her twice daily or more. You will have full responsibility for this dog."

"Oh, Mr. McKenzie, I promise. I promise. Can I bring her home tomorrow after work?" Joey inquired. He already was making plans for her.

"Yes, but you have to pay for the chip and any shots that she needs. Can you handle that?" Harry asked and continued with the house rules of adopting Suzie.

The adoption went well. The first night Suzie didn't sleep in the cage in his room but slept at the foot of Joey's bed after licking Joey's nose.

Joey did well except for one evening when he took Suzie for a walk around the block. The leash slipped out of Joey's hand. Every time Joey told Suzie to come, she ran farther away. By the time he got home with Suzie, the residents were finishing dinner and almost ready to do dishes. Everyone told him how worried they were about him and Suzie as it got later and later. After that incident, Joey and Suzie didn't get separated again.

Within the next two months Joey got put on full-time hours and with the help of Jimbo and Harry, moved his belongings into his own apartment with Suzie. Everyone congratulated Joey on his accomplishments and told him they would miss him and Suzie at the breakfast table each morning.

After the fundraiser for the second shelter, Mr. Fleming encouraged his office crew to match his personal $2,500 pledge to Harry's fund for operating the shelter. The more Mr. Fleming spoke the more an idea grew in Mr. Johnson's mind about maybe serving on the executive board of directors of Harry's homeless shelter program in addition to matching Mr. Fleming's pledge. Each week it seemed the idea grew more important for him to be a part of such a helpful and successful enterprise.

One afternoon between cases Mr. Johnson finally decided to call Harry. As the phone was ringing, he came to the decision to ask him out to lunch. It would provide an opportunity to talk privately. A voice interrupted the ringing with, "Good afternoon. Homeless Shelter. This is Harry."

"Harry, this is Mr. Johnson from Fleming & Johnson. I haven't spoken with you in a while and thought I would give you a call."

"Sure, it is good to hear from you. How are you doing?" Harry asked as he thought, "Oh, No! I wonder if he found something wrong with my finances with the fundraiser. Could he be trying to be further trouble to me? A continuation of when I worked there? Maybe, but probably not. I'll be patient and see what he's got to say."

"Harry, I would like to talk to you. I have heard such good reports about your homeless shelter program. I have an idea that I would like to run past you."

Harry's shoulders and mind relaxed as he realized it was a friendly call after all.

"Are you free tomorrow for lunch? Could you meet me at

the Country Club? It would be my treat. You select what time would be good for you. I'm available anytime between 12:00 and 2:00 p.m."

"Why sure, I can hardly wait to hear your idea. I'll meet you there about noon," he offered.

"Perfect, see you there." And, the phone went silent.

"That was an abrupt ending. I hope everything is okay." Harry mused. With Mr. Johnson, one never knew.

At noon the next day, Harry confidently walked into the club as he did the night he celebrated his promotion at the law firm. He spotted Mr. Johnson. This time Mr. Johnson seemed to be the one who was eager as he stood and shook hands with Harry. He seemed cordial enough and Harry permitted some of his apprehension to slide off his shoulders and managed to put a genuine smile on his face.

Mr. Johnson was going to wait until after the meal to bring up his idea but found he couldn't wait. So as soon as their waiter took the order to the kitchen, he started right in. "Harry, ever since Mr. Fleming came back from the fundraiser, I have been wanting to be a part of your homeless shelter. I hear Mr. Fleming has been helping you and I want to help too. I would like to provide you with any attorney services you might need for your shelter operations, *pro bono*."

"Since, you would like to help," Harry said, "would you think about becoming a member of my board of directors? It wouldn't take much time as we only meet quarterly. We presently have an opening and I would consider it an honor for you to fill that vacancy." Harry made eye contact to see what Mr. Johnson's reaction might be and watched a smile begin to wreath his face.

"Yes, I have been thinking about that and hoping for just that opportunity. You'll let me know when the next board meeting is?" Mr. Johnson inquired just as their steaming hot meal arrived.

At the first board meeting that Mr. Johnson attended Harry provided him with a listing of all the individuals who had gone through his shelter to date. Included was a former resident named Roy. Mr. Johnson immediately spoke up and asked, "Could his last name be Johnson? I have a son named Roger that I haven't seen or heard from in almost eight years. He had the nickname, Roy. We parted under very stressful conditions which I regret. He stopped all contact with me and left no clues to his whereabouts so I couldn't find him when I tried. If this could possibly be him, I would love to make arrangements to see him again if he is willing. Hopefully he is in the area and it could be arranged."

"You may be in luck, Mr. Johnson. I recall when Roy signed our shelter application, he listed J.D. Johnson as his third reference. I think it is your son. He went through our program and has been hired permanently and full time with the Evansville School System in the maintenance department. He recently volunteered and helped out with the fundraiser, and I think he was hoping you might attend," Harry commented.

"How is he doing? Does he look healthy? What is his demeanor? When he was living at home, he fought with me and his mother almost all the time." Eager for the answers he intently looked at Harry.

"Mr. Johnson, you'll be glad to know he is doing well at work and even has his own retirement plan and health insurance and his own apartment. I'll tell you what. When I get back to the shelter, I'll check with him about giving out his cell phone number and call you at the office. I can check on his address too.

Harry hadn't completely forgotten how extremely unfairly Mr. Johnson and Mr. Fleming had worked him, but he was so pleased to have him and his expertise on the board of directors of the shelters. Hopefully, his negative feelings of his treatment in the past would fade more and more in time. Harry was very pleased to be where he was now, working with the homeless, more than any other position he had held.

12

True Success

Since leaving the Fleming & Johnson Law Firm on Green River Road so many years ago, Gemme and Harry experienced joy after joy. Harry's health continued to be outstanding with each physical check-up. The only part of his body that hurt was not his heart but his arthritis. As retirement approached, he and Gemme were still living a stress-free life. What a half-a-lifetime of pleasure and fulfillment over the years of helping others. Harry could count the number of sleepless nights on one hand during this time compared to years ago while trying to be a successful lawyer.

As time flew by, the two shelters continuously assisted more homeless until they helped a grand total of one hundred residents over the period of twenty years. With this news some of the faithful backers, donors and loving friends decided to honor Harry and Gemme's fruitful labors during this time with a celebration dinner.

It was almost impossible to keep it a secret from Harry and Gemme. One or two let the surprise slip. Gemme picked up on the unusual scurrying around and was not surprised. The graduates from the shelter pitched in. Although Father O'Malley was no longer the rector at St. Gregory Catholic Church, the parish offered them the use of their fellowship hall. Over the years their fundraisers had filled the hall but this one was going to almost fill it to the point that the fire marshal could have kept people from coming in for safety reasons. The young people who had been servers during the very first fundraiser were now the cooks and directed the celebration.

This time the newspaper and TV reporters were eager to come. It seldom happens that good news gets the front page of the paper or the highlight on the five o'clock news. Well, on this occasion, Harry and Gemme made that climatic point and were featured on the news looking mature and well respected.

During the night of the dinner an offering was taken and a pledge drive was initiated. It was so successful that they were able to buy all new appliances for the shelter kitchens, all new mattresses for the bedrooms and new sinks and cabinets for the bathrooms. They also replaced the bathtubs with new plastic surround showers in both shelters. On top of that, one shelter even got a new roof.

Harry and Gemme were overwhelmed by the generosity of the community. They could hardly believe the wonderful feeling of completeness of their lives of helping others.

The Chamber of Commerce took advantage of this promotion to get the City of Evansville to build their own homeless shelter. The Chamber worked through city council to build a new homeless shelter building completely paid for by the city along with federal government grants. This additional homeless shelter didn't diminish Harry and Gemme's shelters' population but was a great asset to the other homeless of Evansville, Indiana.

Soon after it was completed there was a city-wide dedication of Evansville's new homeless shelter. The mayor spoke praising the McKenzies, "It's an honor for me to speak today at this luncheon. I've become closely acquainted with Harry and Gemme. I have become particularly close to Harry over the years. He exhibits a spirit of contentment, and he daily exhibits an aura of true success. I am proud of our hometown boy who has made a notable impact on our fair city. Harry has helped us gain a reputation as a town that takes care of its homeless persons.

He has not only helped many homeless during his life but now the City of Evansville will be able to for a long time. It is my extreme delight to officially name this 1.7-million-dollar homeless center built with City of Evansville funds the 'Harry McKenzie Building' in lasting tribute to our exemplary Evansville Citizen."

"Let's put our hands together in appreciation for Harry McKenzie, the gray-haired man with a ready smile, and his industrious wife, Gemme," the mayor concluded. In unison, the audience rose and gave them a long-lasting round of applause.

After most guests had exited Harry sauntered over to Gemme and gently put his arm around her and said, "Let's go home, Honey." She gave him a nice smile and realized again that since they left the law office, they had achieved true success.